Love's Truth

By the Author

Edge of Awareness

The Courage to Try

Imperfect Truth

Love Came Calling

Through Love's Eyes

Love's Truth

Visit us at www.boldstrokesbooks.com

Love's Truth

by
C.A. Popovich

2021

LOVE'S TRUTH
© 2021 By C.A. Popovich. All Rights Reserved.

ISBN 13: 978-1-63555-755-8

This Trade Paperback Original Is Published By
Bold Strokes Books, Inc.
P.O. Box 249
Valley Falls, NY 12185

First Edition: March 2021

This is a work of fiction. Names, characters, places, and incidents are the product of the author's imagination or are used fictitiously. Any resemblance to actual persons, living or dead, business establishments, events, or locales is entirely coincidental.

This book, or parts thereof, may not be reproduced in any form without permission.

Credits
Editors: Victoria Villaseñor and Stacia Seaman
Production Design: Stacia Seaman
Cover Design by Tammy Seidick

Acknowledgments

The idea for this book, as do many of mine, came from my local news. A couple went to Hawaii and left their kids behind. It turned out that they were involved in a cult in Idaho and no one knew where their kids were. I'm not sure how it all ended because the story faded away as they often do to be replaced by more recent news.

I decided to make one of my characters a survivor of a cult, and my research began on the internet where I found *Escaping Utopia*, by Janja Lalich and Karla McLaren, published by Routledge Taylor & Francis group. It is a wonderful resource for anyone interested in reading real-life stories of people who've escaped from cults.

My book is fiction, a love story based on my imagination and characters I made up. I hope readers enjoy the adventure, feel the joy of falling in love, and find a moment of escape.

I want to express my continued appreciation for all the hardworking, awesome folks at Bold Strokes Books for giving my stories a home and the fantastic editors, Victoria and Stacia, who help me make the story so much better.

I also want to thank my friend Sandi for her feedback on my first draft.

To love.

Prologue

Matthew's Faith Hideout, remote area of Idaho

Sarah crouched in a corner next to the only door in the room as she forced her breathing to normal and struggled to still her shaking hands. Her legs ached from the strain of remaining in one position. Brother Matthew addressed the group as he poured clear liquid into the grape juice in their communion jug. "Holy water," her mother had told her, but at twenty-four she knew better than to believe it. He raised the jug with one hand and his other, palm up, toward the ceiling.

"Today will be our final communion, my flock." He lifted the bottle higher and closed his eyes. "This blessed jug contains nourishment for our salvation. It's time for the spiritual union that will bind us together forever. It will be our righteous path to show our sacred trust. The moment of faith. Our rebirth!"

It was now or never. She glanced at the guard who'd raised his hands and eyes to the ceiling, and she slipped out the door and ran.

Chapter 1

Wisconsin Dells, twelve years later

Barb Donnelly relaxed in the lounge chair and gazed at the flowing waters of the Wisconsin River below her. Grateful she'd spent the extra money for this room with the waterfront view, she closed her eyes to absorb the peace and quiet of the first vacation she'd taken in five years. She loved her job as a conservation officer in the Upper Peninsula of Michigan, but she needed this break. She took a deep breath and released it before heading to the hotel dining area for breakfast. She waited for the young man in front of her to receive his order and accepted the plate with the cheese and spinach omelet from the server with the most gorgeous sparkling blue eyes she'd ever seen. Her pulse rate quickened, and she stood captivated long enough for the elderly couple behind her to whisper their impatience. "Sorry," she mumbled.

She smiled at the server and forced herself not to stare before settling at one of the small tables by a window. Barb watched the woman create custom omelets while she smiled but didn't engage much with anyone. She concentrated on her breakfast while sneaking glances at the dark-haired, blue-eyed beauty. It seemed perhaps this vacation held more promise than only relaxation. She finished eating and refilled her coffee cup, reluctant to leave without finding out more about the woman who'd captured her attention so completely. Barb wasn't shy and had no reservations about approaching an attractive woman, but this woman was working, and Barb respected that boundary. She settled back into her chair, sipped coffee, and waited until the woman began to clean up her area before going to stand near the omelet station.

"Thank you for the great omelet this morning." Barb smiled. "My name's Barb." She hoped the woman would offer her name, but she stood silent and looked around before leveling her attention on Barb. Barb relaxed, unmoving, and allowed her to assess. Her need to be found worthy surprised her for a moment.

"My name's Lynette, and I'm glad you enjoyed your breakfast." She didn't look away but remained quiet.

Lynette knew as much about her as she did the twenty other strangers seated throughout the room, and Barb intended to change that. "If you're finished working, would you have a cup of coffee with me?" Barb hoped to put Lynette at ease, so she smiled again.

"I have to put all these dishes away." She hesitated and looked toward the kitchen.

"I'll wait for you."

Lynette gave her a quick smile and then turned away with her armful of dishes. Barb settled back into her seat and hoped Lynette would join her, but after an hour, she decided Lynette wasn't interested, so she left.

"Is the coffee offer still good?" Lynette stood in the hallway outside the dining area, like she'd been waiting for her.

"Absolutely. Do you want to stay in the dining room? Or my balcony has a fantastic view, if you'd like to get away from the kitchen." Barb knew she was on the edge of being forward, but something in Lynette's demeanor intrigued her and tugged at her sense of protectiveness.

Lynette seemed to deliberate. "I love all the different views from this hotel. I'll get us a couple of coffees and be right back." She disappeared into the kitchen.

Barb leaned against the wall next to the exit to wait for Lynette and watched people outside talking and gesturing. Probably making plans for their day's excursions. Wisconsin Dells had boat trips, zip lines, and waterparks to explore, but all she wanted at this moment was to spend time getting to know Lynette. She sensed her shyness, and Barb didn't want to push her, but the spark she'd felt when their eyes first met left her wanting to know more about her. Drummond Island, where Barb lived, wasn't exactly a lesbian mecca, and it had been a long time since she'd felt anything close to the attraction she felt now. She hoped she'd have time to explore their possible connection, and really hoped Lynette agreed.

Lynette let Claudia know she was taking her break and packed two coffees, packets of sugar and creamer, and several varieties of muffins into a paper bag. She took a few minutes to double-check her reflection in the restroom mirror. She'd been asked out by several men in the years she'd worked at the hotel, but Barb was the first female to show any interest in her. It was a nice change. She pushed away her eagerness. Slow was the safe way to go. The dining area had been full for this early in the season, but Barb had grabbed her attention the moment she'd taken a seat next to the window. She'd had to force herself to concentrate on her cooking and ignore Barb's soft smile and confident demeanor. She took a deep, settling breath before proceeding to the lobby. Sharing coffee with a new friend was all this was. Barb stood staring out the glass entry door, so she stopped to observe her for a moment. She stood a couple inches taller than Lynette and the morning sun reflected off her thick auburn hair. Her snug jeans and T-shirt showed off her toned physique. Gorgeous and sexy came to mind, but when Barb turned her hazel eyes on her, all coherent thoughts fled. She faltered when Barb smiled, and her fingers grazed the top of her hand as she reached to help her carry the bag.

"This feels like more than a couple cups of coffee."

"I thought we could share a few of the leftover muffins. That's okay, isn't it?" Lynette squeezed her fingers into her palm, her attempt to remind herself she didn't need to apologize or ask permission for everything. She'd gotten better at reading people, and she hoped her first perception of Barb would hold true. She hadn't had a new friend in her life in a long time.

"It's great. Thanks for thinking of it. I'm on the fourth floor."

Lynette tried to relax as she followed Barb to her suite. Barb seemed nice, and they were only going to share coffee and muffins and the view from her balcony. It would be safe enough as long as she stayed relaxed and kept the focus on Barb.

"Here we are." Barb opened the door and stepped aside for her.

Lynette went straight to the balcony and set the bag on the small table between two lounge chairs. "You're right. This is a great view." Barb must have paid top dollar for this room. She hadn't been to this side of the hotel in years, but most of the wealthiest guests usually booked rooms here. Barb didn't seem to fit the persona of the moneyed folks she'd met.

"Let's sit. I'd like to get to know you." Barb took the coffees out and set one on each side of the bag before taking a sip from one.

"Did you see the creamer and sugar in the bag?"

"Yeah. Thanks. I take mine black." Barb removed the muffins from the bag and set them on napkins on the small table. "Thanks for bringing all this." She picked out a blueberry muffin and took a bite. "Have you worked at the hotel long?" she asked.

"About six years." Lynette chose a cinnamon muffin and settled onto a chair before breaking off a piece and popping it into her mouth. Deflection was second nature now, but then, most people were happy to talk about themselves, and that made it easier.

"This is the first time I've been here. I decided it was time for a vacation, so here I am. I'm glad I chose this hotel with this view, and meeting you is especially nice."

Lynette felt the blush creep up her neck to her cheeks. She'd been in the background for so long she'd forgotten what it felt like to be noticed, especially by an attractive woman. She took a sip of coffee and watched the sun sparkle off the water while she struggled to come up with a reply. The peaceful scene was nothing like the churning in her gut. It had been years since she'd felt an attraction like this. It was dangerous, and yet she didn't want to leave. She could give herself this, just for a moment.

Chapter 2

"I'll finish prepping for tomorrow's brunch and head home." Lynette spoke to her coworker and friend, Claudia, as she arranged items in the refrigerator. The routine work did little to keep her mind off her coffee chat with Barb. The ease with which Barb talked about herself and her life stirred her to tell stories of her weird encounters with guests at the hotel. She'd vowed never to get close to anyone again after her second and last attempt at a relationship, so she'd carefully avoided any personal information. And there was her past. Not even someone seemingly as easygoing as Barb would accept that. She finished her work and tried to leave her lingering apprehensions behind as she concentrated on the drive home. She pulled into her carport and smiled in anticipation of the greeting she knew awaited her as she walked to her apartment door.

"Whoa, Starr." Lynette's dog's whole body quivered with excitement, and her tail wagged like a windshield wiper on high as she bounced and whined in front of her. "Let me get past the door." She dropped to the floor and Starr settled into her lap. Lynette held her until her heart rate slowed and a sense of calm replaced any tension brought on by thoughts of her past. She rose and opened her door to watch Starr race to her potty area and return to face her. "Let's go check out the park." She fastened on Starr's Therapy Dog halter and clipped on her leash, then grabbed her fleece top and headed to her favorite path. The winding route took them along a shallow river and a mile through two stands of hardwoods. She loved this time of year. The spring leaves and abundant undergrowth evidenced continuation of life. She breathed in the fresh air and pushed aside memories of sweltering days and freezing nights. She reached down, and Starr raised her head to meet her touch and kept her focused on the present. Her warmth and soft fur grounded her, and she ran her fingers over her ears as she concentrated on gratitude. "Let's get home." Lynette stepped up her pace for a dose of exercise, and her breath caught on long-suppressed memories of forced marches barefoot through hot sand in the noonday sun.

"Sacrifice and dedication to the avoidance of slothfulness," Brother Matthew had said.

Starr whined and glued herself to her side. "I thought I was over this," she murmured in Starr's ear and wiped tears from her face. Her therapist had told her flashbacks could linger for a lifetime but would probably lessen with time. "How much time?" she muttered. Lynette reminded herself how far she'd come, inhaled the cool evening air, and continued home.

"I haven't forgotten." Lynette grinned at Starr sitting next to her food bowl. She filled her bowl and made herself a cup of hot chocolate before she settled on her couch with her phone. Her aunt answered on the second ring.

"Hello, honey."

Lynette could always count on her aunt to be there for her. "Hi, Aunt Jen. How're you doing?"

"I'm good. I've cut down on my hours at work to spend more time on my art."

"I miss you." Lynette had missed her biweekly visit due to changes in her work schedule.

"I miss you, too. Do you think you'll have time next week?"

"I plan to make time. I want to see your new exhibit at the gallery. Is everything quiet?" Quiet was their code for no word from Lynette's mother, her aunt's sister.

"All quiet. The way we like it. And my gallery isn't going anywhere, but I'd love to see you."

Lynette told her aunt about work and how Starr was doing before promising to visit soon. She hadn't told her aunt about meeting Barb, and she wondered why the thought even crossed her mind to do so. It was a chat over coffee, nothing more. She was a woman on vacation, and she'd be gone soon. There was nothing to tell.

Lynette made herself another cup of hot chocolate and relaxed on her couch with Starr. She'd lived with her aunt until she felt prepared to live on her own after fleeing the cult. Her aunt had saved her life, and Lynette would be forever grateful. She planned to celebrate her aunt's upcoming sixtieth birthday but hadn't decided how yet. "Let's make a list, Starr." She picked up a scratch pad and pencil and began a list of her aunt's favorite food items to buy for dinner. She had seating for six at her dining room table, but she realized she didn't really have anyone to invite. Maybe her aunt had a friend or two Lynette hadn't met. She sighed, finished her hot chocolate, and got ready for bed. She tossed and turned for half an hour before using her therapist's advice and meditating until she fell asleep.

Lynette awoke to Starr's whine and the feel of her pressed against her side. Bits and pieces of her nightmare floated to her consciousness. She hadn't dreamt of her parents in years. The bad dream involved her mother slapping her and declaring her faith lacking because her arranged marriage hadn't produced any offspring to increase the number of followers for the *anointed one*. Her father shunned her by turning his back to her and declaring her dead to them. She pulled Starr close and allowed the heat of her body and the rise and fall of her chest as she breathed to comfort her. She gave up on any more sleep that night.

Starr followed close when she rose to set up her coffeepot and settle on her couch to do the deep breathing and meditation her therapist had taught her. She took a few minutes to reflect on her fears. She knew they were probably unwarranted, but they remained very real to her. Until she was able to put her past where it belonged, they'd haunt her and she would never be able to let an interesting woman like Barb into her life. She rested her hand on Starr's back to settle her angst, knowing she would never subject anyone to the danger of her life. "It's just you and me, sweetie." She buried her face in Starr's fur and let the tears fall.

Chapter 3

Barb watched the tour boat full of passengers glide across the water. She wanted to take the tour, but she didn't really want to do it alone. It seemed like everything she did these days outside work, she did alone. The few friends she had were either married or too busy with their lives to have much time to spend with her. Then there was the fact that her idea of fun was trekking through the woods or relaxing on the water with a fishing pole. She'd found most single women wanted more out of a date. She'd enjoyed the short time they'd spent together and sensed a connection she hoped Lynette had felt, too, although she didn't want to come across as some kind of creep. Lynette seemed very private and shy, and Barb hoped she could break through her reticence. She perused the many pamphlets highlighting the area's events and enjoyed the peaceful view for a few minutes before she headed to the dining area for breakfast.

"Good morning." Barb smiled at Lynette as she folded Barb's omelet onto a plate.

"Good morning. Did you have a pleasant sleep?"

"I did. I love being anywhere near water, and the room was peaceful and quiet. Did you sleep well?" Barb glanced at the line behind her and realized she couldn't take as much time as she'd like to talk to Lynette.

"I'll stop by your table after I'm done here and we can talk, if that's okay?"

"Sounds great. See you when you're done." Barb enjoyed her omelet and sipped her coffee while she waited.

"Hey. Sorry it took so long. I had to put the leftovers away, but I've got a ten-minute break now." She set four muffins on the table and settled in the seat across from Barb with her coffee.

"Thanks for the muffins." Barb chose a blueberry and smiled at the thoughtful gesture. "I want to ask you something." She set a pamphlet on the table between them. "I want to take this sunset dinner cruise while I'm here, and I really don't want to go alone. What do you think?" She pushed the brochure toward Lynette.

She glanced at the leaflet and smiled. "I've been before, and it's nice."

"Great. When would you be available?"

Lynette bit her lip and stared at the brochure for a long moment. "I have to stop home to feed my dog first."

Barb heard the hesitation in her voice and wondered if she'd made a mistake asking. "I'll see if I can get tickets for tonight. It'll be fun." She waited, expecting her to decline. Lynette took a deep breath and seemed to wrestle with a decision.

Finally, she nodded slightly. "Shall I meet you back here?"

"Sure. I'll get the tickets. Do you have a cell?"

"I do." Lynette paused. "But I don't actually give the number out. I'm sorry."

"No problem. I totally get it." Barb was careful who she gave her number to, so she understood Lynette's reluctance. "But I'll give you mine, just in case you can't make it." She wrote it on a napkin and Lynette tucked it in her pocket.

"I should be back in plenty of time."

"Come hungry. Surf and turf is on the menu. I'll see you later. And, Lynette?"

"Yes?"

"I'm looking forward to spending the evening with you." Barb gently touched Lynette's wrist before leaving. She walked along the river for a few minutes before getting their tickets. Was it her imagination, or had Lynette stiffened a little at her touch? Some people didn't like casual touch, but Barb often reached out to people. She liked the contact and thought touch often conveyed what words sometimes couldn't. Still, Lynette had agreed to come along, and that was something.

Barb relaxed in her balcony chair with a novel, enjoying the breeze on her face. The thought of having Lynette's company tonight made her smile. It had been a long time since she'd relaxed with someone over dinner, and there was nothing wrong with a little vacation romance, if it came to that. And even if it didn't, it was still nice to have something to look forward to.

She set her book aside, then took a shower and dressed before heading downstairs to find Lynette. She paused outside the hotel dining room to appreciate the view of the river before entering the room.

"Hey there." Lynette smiled, but her eyes darted here and there, like she was watching for something.

"Hi. Are we ready?" Lynette had changed into white slacks and a royal blue blouse that highlighted her beautiful eyes. She was gorgeous.

"Yes. Let's go cruising."

"Did you have enough time to get home and feed your dog?"

"Yes. She'll be fine for a while now."

"Good. I love this walk along the water." Barb jammed her hands in her pockets to keep from reaching for Lynette's hand as they ambled toward the dock. "Have you lived near here long?"

Lynette took a long minute to answer. "A few years."

Barb rested her hand on Lynette's lower back as they walked up the ramp onto the boat, but took it away immediately when she felt Lynette stiffen under her touch. "Do you mind if we sit on the west side? I'd love to watch the sunset reflect off the wake." Barb pointed to an empty table.

"I like the side seats, too," Lynette said.

Barb squelched a tingle of desire as she watched the blush

creep up Lynette's neck to her cheeks. She was lovely. She sat opposite her and sipped from her plastic water cup. "I'm glad you agreed to do this with me."

"I'm glad you asked me. I told you I'd been once before, but it was only a short trip, and I didn't have dinner. I'm looking forward to the surf and turf." Lynette rested her forearms on the table and wrapped her hands around her water cup.

Lynette's delicate hands and long fingers distracted Barb so that she missed what she said.

"Is that okay?" Lynette tipped her head and smiled.

"Sorry. I missed what you said." Barb could feel the heat rise up her neck.

"I asked if you were going to have a glass of wine. I'd like one, if you are. I'm not one to drink alone, though."

"Sounds good." Barb sipped her wine after it was delivered and decided to try to get Lynette to open up to her. "So, you have a dog, you work at the hotel, and you like coffee. Do you live nearby?"

Lynette took a sip of her wine before speaking. "Not too far. I have an apartment a few miles south of here."

Their conversation was interrupted by the server. The plates set before them were piled high with lobster and filet mignon along with corn on the cob and biscuits, and the side salad looked fresh. "This is a lot of food," Barb said.

"It looks great." Lynette spoke around a mouthful of lobster.

Barb smiled, pleased at Lynette's enthusiasm. "It does." She took a bite of her steak. "This is delicious." She swallowed before speaking again. "Do you have any family in the area?"

Lynette set her fork down and stared at her plate. "I have an aunt not far from here, but that's it."

"No brothers or sisters?"

"Nope. Just me."

"Have you always lived in Wisconsin?"

"My whole adult life. I lived with my aunt for a while until I started my job at the hotel."

"Do you like to read?"

"I do, but I don't usually take the time to. I never got into the habit, I guess." Lynette shrugged and took a bite of her food.

Nothing more was forthcoming, and it felt like she was grilling her with questions, so she remained quiet and concentrated on the meal and the view along the river. Barb watched Lynette set her fork aside, take a sip of wine, and take a deep breath before picking up her fork to continue to eat. She wondered if she wasn't enjoying the meal. "Is everything good?"

"It's great." She looked down at her plate then up. "I tend to eat way too fast. As a kid…well…I had to or it would be taken away." She continued to eat. "So I try to slow down now."

Barb made a mental note to revisit that piece of information at a later date. She moved on to lighter topics and told a few anecdotes about work that had Lynette laughing. It was a lovely sound and reminded Barb just how long it had been since she'd wined and dined a beautiful woman. And although Lynette clearly had boundaries, it was still a fantastic evening. When they parted at the hotel, Barb had hesitated, wondering if she could lean in for a kiss, but Lynette had backed up and waved, and that was that. It didn't stop her from smiling all the way back to her room, though.

Chapter 4

Lynette couldn't remember a time she'd spontaneously broken into a smile, but she found herself smiling as she drove home after her dinner date with Barb. She pulled into her carport, shut off the car engine, and rested her head on the headrest. She closed her eyes and allowed the comfort being with Barb evoked to wash over her. She could still feel the heat of her hand on her back as they'd boarded the boat. The casual touch had felt strange at first, but when Barb pulled her hand away, she'd missed the feeling. She allowed herself a brief memory of the last woman she'd trusted with her heart. She'd never do it again. Barb seemed tender, kind, and compassionate, but Lynette needed to be vigilant. She'd worked too hard to heal to allow anyone to upset her serenity. Something told her Barb wouldn't be dangerous, but she couldn't take a chance. They'd shared a pleasant dinner cruise and it gave her an opportunity to practice her conversation skills. An enjoyable evening was enough. She climbed out of her car and locked the doors, content with her decision and grateful for a chance to be with someone who made her laugh, even if it was temporary.

"I'm home," Lynette called out. Her chest constricted with fear for the few seconds it took Starr to appear from around the corner and greet her. She might be healing from her past, but she still needed her therapy dog. Starr was her second one, and she'd never be without one. "Hey, you lazy bump." She dropped to the floor and hugged her while Starr rested her head on her shoulder. When her heart stopped thumping, she stood and opened the door to let Starr outside to take care of business while she made a cup of hot chocolate.

"Hey, girl. I have a new friend." Lynette sat on her couch with Starr curled next to her. She rarely allowed herself memories of her life before the cult and was unsure why they arose now. But there was no question they were lurking in the back of her mind, and images of that time kept popping up like evil clowns. She was twelve when her parents moved them to the compound in the desert. She'd had a couple of friends who had been neighbors and fellow home-schooled kids, and she often wondered what they thought about her sudden disappearance. She sighed away the memories and hugged Starr, who had sensed her discomfort and rested her head in her lap.

"It's bedtime, sweetie." Starr hopped off the couch and Lynette let her outside before changing into her pajamas. She closed her eyes and meditated away more unpleasant memories, but not before they'd already drained the energy from her body. Starr returned, and Lynette welcomed the dreamless sleep as soon as her head hit the pillow.

Lynette woke to the jiggle of the bed as Starr jumped off. She glanced at her alarm clock and followed her to the back door. "How do you always do this two minutes before my alarm goes off?" She set up her coffeemaker, let Starr in, and went to get ready for work.

She enjoyed her job at the hotel. People came and went, and they rarely really looked at the people who worked there. Anonymity had kept her safe all these years, and it made life calm. Cooking was therapeutic, too, and she barely gave most guests a cursory, polite glance throughout the day. That was her life, and although Barb had found a crack in the wall, she couldn't let that crack go any further.

"Good morning." Her boss met her at the entrance to the kitchen, looking as harried and grumpy as he usually did. "I need you to cover for Claudia this morning. She won't be in until noon." He turned and disappeared into the storage room off the back of the kitchen without another word.

Lynette shrugged off his abruptness and concentrated on her routine of preparing the room for the guests. Her life experience had taught her to keep her head down and expect the worst. She walked the perimeter of the room, confident everything was ready, and settled in at her station to wait for the first omelet order. She had a job to do and she'd do it to the best of her ability.

"Swiss cheese and spinach, please." Barb held her plate out in front of her.

"Morning. One omelet coming up." Lynette smiled, unaccountably happy to see Barb.

"Will you be able to have coffee with me later?" Barb asked.

She should say no. Put a stop to this now before she slipped up. "I'm not sure. My coworker will be in late today, and I'll probably have to start the lunch buffet."

"I'll check with you later, then." Barb took her plate to her table.

It was good that she hadn't pushed, and she was able to relax and concentrate again for the rest of her shift. Lynette waited for the few stragglers to finish before she began to put away the breakfast food. Barb's request to share a coffee made her smile, and she put two blueberry muffins in a take-out bag. She noted Barb wasn't at her table and the stab of disappointment surprised her, even though she knew it was better this way. She finished prepping everything for lunch and waited for Claudia to arrive while squelching her desire to go in search of Barb.

Lynette waited until the last minute before giving up on Claudia's arrival. She refilled the coffeepot and prepared the warming pans for the lunch menu. She finished as her boss called her into his office.

"I got a call from Claudia. She'll be off for a few days. You'll be working all three shifts." He bent over his laptop, clearly dismissing her.

Extra shifts meant extra pay, but it would leave her less free time. It would upset her routine, and she hated that. And her desire to spend at least some time with Barb surprised, and worried, her. She worked steadily and refilled pans as they emptied. She readied the dinner menu between refilling the coffee urn, grateful for Claudia's organization. She followed her recipe for chicken and dumplings and put water to boil for potatoes. Thoughts of Barb only interfered a few times, and she buried them under the dirty dishes. There was no room for complication in her life.

Chapter 5

Barb propped her feet on the railing of her balcony and reviewed the brochure highlighting the attractions in the area. She decided the day's adventure would include the Cave of the Mounds, and she hoped Lynette would go with her, although she'd seemed distant when she'd asked her to join her for coffee. Maybe she was busy. She said the hotel was shorthanded, and while Barb was on vacation, it wasn't like she could expect Lynette to drop everything to hang out with her. She watched the water for a while before going to lunch.

"Hi there." Barb smiled at the unexpected presence of Lynette standing at her table. "Are you working?"

"Yeah. Claudia, my coworker, will be off for a few days, so I'm the backup."

"Ah. Will you have any time for a break later?"

Lynette sighed. "I'll take a break after I clean up from the lunch, but I'll have to be back to cover the dinner buffet."

"Sounds perfect. What shall I get for your break on my balcony?" Barb hoped Lynette would agree.

"There's usually leftovers from lunch I can bring, if that's okay? I probably won't have time to eat until then. And if you have hot chocolate, I'll be content."

"Hot chocolate it is." The Cave of the Mounds could wait. She looked forward to spending time with Lynette. She finished half a sandwich to hold her over and a cup of coffee before she went to search for hot chocolate and wait for Lynette.

Barb watched the boat filled with people cruise slowly on the river tour below her. She sipped from her bottle of Coke and relaxed. This was the perfect place for her much-needed vacation, and Lynette agreeing to spend time with her made it special. She'd found hot chocolate after checking several stores, and she looked forward to Lynette's company. She perused the magazine with the area attractions listed and wondered what Lynette might enjoy. She'd enjoyed the sunset dinner cruise. Would she like the riding stables? Or maybe one of the renowned water parks? Barb didn't care about the zip line tours, and her impression was Lynette wouldn't either. Wondering about it all frustrated her. Lynette still seemed like she'd run away if Barb pushed. She'd have to take things slowly and hope she could gain Lynette's trust. She checked the time before filling the small coffeemaker in the room with water. She didn't know how long a break Lynette had, so she planned to have the hot chocolate ready when she arrived. She settled on a chair and chuckled at herself. She knew very little about Lynette except that she was attracted to her. She could be a friendly hotel worker with a couple of kids and an ex-husband, but Barb doubted the husband part. She'd said she lived in an apartment with her dog. Surely she would've mentioned children if she had any. The best thing to do would be to ask her directly and not push for more than Lynette wanted to give.

"Hello," Lynette called as she knocked on the door.

"Come on in," Barb said. "I'm out on the balcony." She'd propped the door open a crack for her.

Lynette set a bag of leftover lunch food on the small table between the chairs. "I brought turkey sandwiches and coleslaw."

Lynette smiled and Barb lost herself in the sparkle of her eyes. She shook herself and rose to retrieve the hot chocolate.

Lynette took a sip and set the cup down. "Yum. I got hooked

on it the first time I had it ten years ago." She took the sandwiches out of the bag and placed them on napkins on the table.

"Thanks for all this." Barb took a bite of her sandwich. "I didn't eat a big lunch in anticipation of eating with you instead." This was the second tidbit of information she put away for review. Food taken away as a child and hot chocolate only discovered ten years ago. Lynette intrigued her, but she sensed she'd flee as fast as a jackrabbit if she pushed for information. "How long can you stay?"

Lynette looked at her watch. "Half an hour."

"Cool. When we finish eating, I'd like to get your opinion on what's best to do here."

"I'm probably not the best person for that information. I pretty much come to work and go home. The only reason I went on the boat cruise once was because Claudia didn't want to go by herself."

Barb took a drink of Coke for time to organize her thoughts. She hadn't asked Lynette if she was seeing anyone. She didn't even know for sure she was a lesbian, although she was pretty sure she was. Maybe she and Claudia were a couple. She was still thinking about how to ask when Lynette spoke.

"I don't do much after work except walk my dog in the park near my apartment." Lynette took a bite of her sandwich and settled back into her chair with her hands wrapped around her cup of hot chocolate.

"So, no one special in your life?"

"Just Starr. She's my golden retriever." She took a drink of her hot chocolate.

"I used to have a dog until my hours got so unpredictable. I felt bad leaving him alone so much," Barb said.

"What kind of dog was he?"

"Badger was a terrier mix. He was a sweet boy but loved to run. I had a heck of a time training him, and it's why I adopted him to a friend. He needed someone with more time to spend with him."

Lynette collected the sandwich wrappers and stuffed them into the bag she'd brought and glanced at her watch. "I think you'd make a good mom for a dog. What do you do, anyway?"

"I'm a conservation officer in Michigan. We're called conservation wardens in Wisconsin, but we do the same thing. Enforce the laws and protect the environment. I love it. Maybe one day I'll get another dog. We'll see." She finished her Coke. "Would you like another cup of hot chocolate?"

"I think I'm good. Thanks. Do you have family?"

"I do. My mom and dad live in South Carolina. Dad is a retired Army general and a Vietnam veteran. My brother is a sergeant in the Michigan State Police department."

"Do you get to see them often?"

"I see Brad, my brother, often, but since my parents live out of state, we only get together for Christmas every year," Barb said. "Do you get to see your aunt often? You said she lives close."

"We get together every couple of weeks, and I talk to her on the phone." Lynette glanced at her watch. "This was nice. Thank you for inviting me, it was good to get away from the kitchen for a little while. Oh, I almost forgot." Lynette pulled out the bag with the blueberry muffins and set it on the table. "For you, later." She smiled.

Barb opened the bag to peek inside. "My favorite. Thank you. I've enjoyed your company. I hope we can do it again. Tomorrow?" She considered the word *company*. A connection she couldn't define and had never felt before drew her to Lynette. Whatever it was wasn't unpleasant, and she wanted more of it.

Lynette stood and looked as if she struggled with the decision. She turned to face her before she spoke. "Can we take this a day at a time? I'm not one for planning ahead, and I've had a couple bad experiences that make me cautious." A blush rose to her cheeks, and she looked away.

Barb took her hands, squeezed gently, and let go. "Of course. Whatever you're comfortable with. Can I walk you back?"

"I'd like that." Lynette visibly relaxed and grabbed the empty bag.

Barb wanted to spend time with Lynette, but she didn't want to scare her away. She'd planned to have all her meals at the hotel so, at least, she could see her at mealtime. She didn't push for more conversation as they took the stairs down to the dining area. She opened the door and Lynette waved before she turned and went to the kitchen.

Barb had time before the dinner buffet, and she was still full from the sandwich and coleslaw, so she took a walk along the river to try to figure out what captivated her about Lynette. She was beautiful, but she'd met many beautiful women and hadn't been drawn to them like she had Lynette. Being with her felt comfortable, but even after three days, she knew very little about her and her life. She really wanted to change that. She mentally shook herself and walked back to her room to change before dinner.

Barb went to her favorite table and hung her jacket over the back of the chair to save it, surprised by the number of people already there. She'd had dinner with Lynette on the riverboat the night before, so she had no idea the hotel's evening buffet was so popular. She filled her plate while keeping an eye out for Lynette. She didn't see her until she set her plate on her table and returned to get an iced tea. She waved and was rewarded with a quick smile and small wave before Lynette turned her attention to refilling pans. Barb decided she'd take Lynette's response as an encouraging sign. She needed to be patient. She had a few more weeks to try to get to know her, and Lynette's disclosure of a couple bad experiences echoed in the back of her mind, warning her to take things slow.

She settled into her chair and enjoyed the view out the window and the variety of people filling their plates and settling at tables to eat. Mostly families and a few singles. She wondered about their stories. It was a fantastic vacation spot with enough natural beauty to satisfy her and plenty of things to do to keep kids and adults entertained. She rarely took time to allow her mind to wander. The knowledge she had nowhere to be or nothing she had to do was a welcome change from her usual demands of being on call and ready for anything. She would've thought she'd be restless and bored, but maybe this vacation thing wasn't so bad. She finished her meal and left to take a walk by the river.

Chapter 6

The rain soaked the ground outside Lynette's sliding glass door, and she loved it. She allowed the memory of rain in the Idaho desert spattering the dry sand and creating tiny puddles the size of the droplets before evaporating to compare with the soaking rain here in Wisconsin. Lynette stepped outside and turned her face to the sky. She breathed in the fresh air and spread her arms to feel the rain on her skin for a few minutes before it was time to get ready for work. Open air and the freedom to revel in it wasn't something she ever took for granted.

She lingered in the hot shower and allowed the water to flow over her head and shoulders. Long hot showers were a daily luxury she allowed herself now. She let herself feel the satisfaction of how far she'd gotten in her healing. She felt deserving of the time she spent caring for herself. She shook off her memories to replace them with thoughts of Barb. She made it clear that she wanted to spend time with her and get to know her. As nice as it would be to be close to someone again, she couldn't pretend there could be anything romantic between them without being hurt or hurting Barb. No. She had to stop any growing feelings now. They'd only met a few days ago, and she couldn't deny how comfortable she felt with her, but Barb was on vacation and would be going home in a few weeks. To consider even a short fling with her would be irresponsible, and she wouldn't do that to anyone. She finished dressing, fed Starr, and left for work. She pulled into the parking lot a few minutes early and noticed Claudia's car parked in her usual spot. She hurried into the building.

"Hi, Claudia. I'm glad you're back, but I thought you were gone for a few days." Lynette stored her purse in her locker and joined Claudia at the omelet station.

"I'll tell you all about it later," Claudia whispered while she looked toward their boss's office.

"We'll talk after the rush. You want the omelet station?" Lynette asked.

"Yeah. Thanks."

Lynette retreated to the kitchen and began cooking potatoes and bacon for the warming pans. She checked the supply of waffles next to the toaster and stopped when she saw Barb smiling her gorgeous smile at Claudia. She watched Barb shift her plate to her right hand to accept the omelet, a move she'd gotten used to seeing, and forced away the desire to rush between them to draw Barb's attention. She took a deep breath and returned to the kitchen. She'd learned about feelings of attachment in the cult and it had been disastrous. Lynette's feeling when she saw Barb paying attention to Claudia was more akin to what she felt when Ruth told her she was pregnant with Brother Matthew's child, and they were no longer going to spend nights together. What she felt now was uncomfortable and confusing. Her aunt had worked with Lynette's therapist to help her identify feelings, but even after so many years, she still had a hard time deciding if her feelings were appropriate. There was certainly no place for feelings of any kind toward Barb, given that they barely knew one another. She took a deep breath to settle herself and went back to prep for the breakfast crowd.

"Good morning." Barb's voice drifted into the kitchen from the doorway.

Lynette turned to face Barb and all her angst dissolved. "Good morning." She couldn't think of anything else to say.

"I met your friend, Claudia, this morning. She seems nice. Since she's back, will you have time for a visit on my balcony this morning?"

Lynette put down the spoon she was holding and took a breath before speaking. "I'll let you know. Okay?" She hadn't heard Claudia's story yet, and now she hoped it wasn't a long one.

"Sounds good. I'll check back with you later."

She watched Barb walk away before turning back to her job. She refilled the pans as they emptied, but her breakfast shift extended due to the weather. The guests lingered over coffee to avoid the rain. She kept an eye on Barb, who seemed to be content to sit at her window seat all day. She watched her refill her coffee and choose a blueberry muffin, and she quickly turned away when Barb caught her and winked.

Claudia had the omelet area cleaned and the cooking equipment put away, so Lynette went to the kitchen to talk to her.

"Hey." She helped her load the industrial dishwasher. "Will you be able to work this afternoon?"

"Yes." She wiped her hands on paper towels. "Did you see the hot woman seated by the window? Her name's Barb, and she's nice. I talked to her this morning."

"I met her the other day. She is nice."

"Yeah? Do you know if she's single?"

Lynette thought for a moment. Barb had asked her to go on the dinner cruise with her, but her experience with women had taught her that assumptions were a bad idea. "I think she is, but I don't know."

"Anyway. I have news. I've applied for a position as a sous-chef at the new Italian restaurant downtown."

Claudia looked excited, so Lynette didn't have the heart to beg her to stay. She'd been working with Claudia for five years, and she was her only friend. "Wow. That's great news. When do you start?" She forced herself not to hold her breath.

"I'm not sure. It would mean more money but probably more

hours. I should hear something by tomorrow. I'd miss working with you. I wanted to let you know what was going on as soon as I came in, but I told the boss I was caring for my sick mother yesterday."

"I'd miss you a lot." Lynette pulled Claudia into a hug, already feeling the loss in the pit of her stomach.

"I'm just working at a different place, I'm not leaving the state. I'll still be here, I promise." Claudia held her at arm's length and smiled.

Lynette relaxed. Her efforts to understand the difference between a friendly hug and sexual expectation took years, and she gratefully accepted Claudia's touch.

Her thoughts quickly turned to Barb and the feelings being with her elicited. Definitely more than only friendly on her part, but did Barb feel the same? It didn't matter. She had no intention of putting herself in the position of being hurt again. She poured herself a cup of coffee and joined Barb at her table.

"Glad you could make it." Barb leaned back in her chair.

"Sorry it took so long. Claudia wanted to talk." Lynette sat opposite her and took a sip of coffee.

"No problem. I'm patient." Barb smiled and held her gaze for a heartbeat before taking a drink of coffee and setting her cup down. "I wanted to ask you something. I'm going to see the Cave of the Mounds tomorrow if it stops raining, and I'd like you to go with me, if you're interested." Barb sipped her coffee and waited.

"Can I let you know tomorrow morning?"

"Sure. I'll be here for breakfast. I'll see you later here for dinner, too." Barb smiled and continued to drink her coffee.

Lynette's knees went weak as she stood to head back to the kitchen. She was in trouble if Barb's simple smile caused that reaction.

Chapter 7

Barb woke to the sound of raindrops hitting the roof over her balcony. Her research before she left home had forecast clear weather for the week, and this was the second day of rain. She rose, put on her robe, and made a cup of coffee. She breathed in the rain-soaked fresh air and felt the swell of gratitude once again she'd chosen this room at the hotel. She had no plans for the day except to make use of the buffets and possibly talk to Lynette, especially now that the cave tour wouldn't happen thanks to the rain.

She finished her coffee and dressed before heading to the dining area, which had become the main focus of her stay. Was that a little sad? She shook her head. It didn't matter. She was on vacation and could do whatever she wanted to. It was a new concept and she was beginning to like it.

The room was filled with early risers getting breakfast and probably waiting for the rain to let up. Barb claimed one of the last available tables and joined the line waiting for omelets. Lynette looked relaxed and smiled at each patron as she set her creations onto their plates. "Good morning." She held out her plate and Lynette placed her omelet in the middle of it.

"Good morning." Lynette smiled and turned to the next person in line.

"Dessert tonight after the dinner hour? It's still raining, so maybe the cave needs to wait till tomorrow." Barb spoke quickly and hesitated for a moment before moving out of the way for the people behind her. Lynette gave her a quick nod, which she interpreted as a yes, and then she picked out an extra piece of cheesecake to take back to her room. She finished breakfast and decided to make the best of the day despite the weather.

Barb put on her rain gear, grabbed her camera, and headed to get photos of the interesting rock formations along the river. She'd read about them in the brochure and wanted to compare them to the shores of Lake Superior. The river streamed below her, and she leaned over the railing to capture shots of the shallow area where it gushed over the rocks. She turned away from the river and watched a couple strolling hand in hand along the road. A stab of loneliness surprised her. She'd thought of herself as independent and content with the life she'd made. She loved her job upholding the laws of her state and protecting the environment, but lately unhappiness with nobody to share her life had seeped in. She didn't know if Lynette was the one to fill the void, but she recognized she very much wanted it filled. The rain let up before noon, and she enjoyed the sunshine for a while before heading back to the hotel.

She started when she entered the dining area and saw a Reserved sign on her table. All the other window seats were taken, so she proceeded to one of the few available tables in the center of the room when Lynette stepped out of the kitchen and walked toward her.

"It's yours." Lynette pointed at the Reserved sign. "Hurry and sit. It's totally forbidden to save tables in here." She rushed back to the kitchen.

Barb went to the table and slipped the paper sign into her pocket before she hung her jacket over the chair and headed to the buffet. Lynette had reserved her favorite table for her, which was incredibly thoughtful and suggested she'd made an impression. Friendly or anything deeper remained to be seen. The dinner cruise had been the longest time they'd spent together so far, and she'd really enjoyed herself. Barb finished her meal and lingered over her coffee, trying to decide if she should remind Lynette about dessert on her balcony. She might scare her away if she pushed too hard, so she went back to her room and hoped Lynette would show up.

The pictures of the rain on the rocks came out better than Barb expected, and she made mental notes regarding the ones she wanted to revisit. She put her camera away and settled on the balcony with a book to wait for Lynette. It was nearly seven p.m. before she heard the knock on the door.

"Am I too late?" Lynette stood outside the door as if expecting to be sent away.

"Never." Barb took her hand and gently tugged her into the room. She hesitated for a heartbeat, trying to read the message in Lynette's eyes before brushing her lips over hers. "I have cheesecake." She feared she'd gone too far, so she released Lynette and stepped back.

"Wow." Lynette blinked at her.

Barb grinned. "I couldn't help myself." She retreated to the coffeemaker, where she had hot water for Lynette's hot chocolate. She turned with a mug in her hand to find Lynette where she'd left her, still looking dazed.

"Do I need to apologize?" Barb hoped she hadn't destroyed any chance with Lynette.

"No. But it took me by surprise." Lynette took the mug and sipped from it. "Thank you."

Barb followed her to the balcony and set the two pieces of cheesecake on the table between them. "I seem to have developed this urge to kiss you every time I see you, but I promise I'll try to keep myself under control. I don't want to do anything to scare you away."

"Like I said, you took me by surprise, and I'm not sure how to respond. I like you, but I definitely need more time before I even begin to think about kissing. Or anything else."

"I understand, and I'm sorry. I'll keep my lips to myself." Damn. She'd moved too fast after all.

"Thanks for the cheesecake. This is one of Claudia's specialties." Lynette took a bite.

"Does Claudia do all the baking?" Barb asked.

"Pretty much. I make a mean omelet, but she's got the talent." Lynette finished her cheesecake in three bites and took a drink of her hot chocolate.

"How long has Claudia been working at the hotel?" Barb asked.

"Almost ten years." Lynette sipped from her mug and didn't say anything else.

"Did you work somewhere else before this hotel?"

"Sort of. I'm from out west, and I worked in a private kitchen out there for years." She continued to sip from her cup, but she looked lost in thought.

"Out west, huh. I've never been farther west than Fargo, North Dakota." Barb didn't want to push for more information than Lynette wanted to give, so she sat back in her chair and remained quiet.

"Idaho," Lynette barely whispered.

"We have a new officer from Boise. It sounds like a pretty state. Mountains and desert." Barb hoped Lynette would elaborate. "The Snake River runs through it, right?"

"Yes. It runs through Twin Falls. I was sort of south of there."

Barb sighed. She considered herself a patient person, but Lynette was the hardest person to get to know she'd ever met. She'd never met someone so unwilling to talk about themselves.

"I'm sorry, Barb. I think I'm being rude, aren't I?"

"No. It's fine, Lyn. Maybe we could repeat the dinner cruise and spend some more time together, or we could go on one of the boat tours or to the waterpark." Barb set her cup down and took Lynette's free hand in hers. "I don't mean to push you. You tell me whatever you're comfortable telling me. I want us to get to know each other while I'm here."

"Are you going home soon?" Lynette sat up and leaned toward her.

"This is the first vacation I've taken in over five years. My chief told me to take at least three weeks. We have a couple of new recruits who are doing a good job taking over for me, so I'm here for three weeks for sure." Barb wasn't certain she'd stay the whole time. She wanted a few days to visit her brother. Her decision would depend on how much interest Lynette showed in her.

Chapter 8

"Nobody's ever called me Lyn before, and I liked it when Barb did." Lynette sat at her kitchen table with Starr at her feet. "Why do you think that is, sweetie?" She rested her hand on Starr's head and felt the calm radiate up her arm to her neck. "She wants to get to know me, and I have to figure out if I want to let her." She drank her coffee and pondered her dilemma. "Maybe I could use her as a test case. She's leaving, so I don't need to worry about long-term complications. But I could learn to open up a little, share myself." She rested her forehead on her folded arms on the table. "What am I going to do? I like her a lot, but two betrayals were enough. I couldn't live through another." She refilled her mug. Lynette finished her coffee and pushed aside more thoughts running through her mind like a broken record. She laughed at herself for speculating, since she had no intention of leading Barb on or putting herself in a vulnerable position. Barb was a new friend who'd be going home in a couple weeks, nothing more. "Let's go for a quick walk before work."

Lynette's heart wanted to trust Barb. Her lips were warm and soft. Her touch was gentle, and she smiled at the memory of their evening together. She had no idea how to reconcile her past with her present. She'd spent years in therapy and worked with a cult survivor group, but so much dysfunction might take her a lifetime to get over. And who would want to be in a relationship with someone so broken? She fed Starr and headed out the door.

She shook off her pondering as she drove to work. She wouldn't put herself in a vulnerable position like she'd already done twice. She'd settled into a job she liked and an apartment where she and Starr were comfortable and close to her aunt. She was safe here and wasn't worried about her past finding her. Initially she'd moved around a lot, worried they'd be looking for her, but here she practically blended into the scenery, which was just the way it should be. Barb would remain a pleasant memory after she went home.

"Good morning, Claudia." Lynette put her purse in her locker and joined Claudia in the kitchen.

"Good morning. Hey, I have a question for you."

"Yeah?"

"I saw you with Barb yesterday. Do you two have a thing going?" Claudia asked.

Lynette scrambled for an answer. She had no idea what their relationship was or where it was going. "We've been talking over the past few days, if that's what you mean."

"I saw the way she looks at you. I think she wants more than only friendship." Claudia leaned against a counter and grinned.

"Did she tell you that?"

"No. She said you were friends, and she was only here for a vacation. Anyway, it's none of my business, but I want you to be happy. Just…be careful with your heart." She pushed off the counter and grabbed a large serving spoon. "I've got the warming pans heated, and the potatoes are almost done."

Lynette went to the restroom for a moment of quiet in an attempt to settle the uncertainty gurgling in her gut. She wanted something with Barb, but she didn't know what, and she didn't want to lead her on. She raised her fingers to her lips. They still tingled from Barb's brief velvety kiss. She suppressed the unwelcome craving, took a deep breath, and decided to stick with friendship. Friends talked and spent time together, but friends also shared who they were with each other. Could she offer that vulnerability to Barb? Could she handle even friendship with her? It would be fairer than anything more, but Barb would be leaving in a few weeks, so why should she bother? Claudia's words echoed in her mind. *Be careful with your heart.* No solid answers came to her, so she made a mental note to make a therapy appointment and left to help Claudia prep for breakfast.

She checked the pans as the guests made their way from one to the next and refilled them as they emptied while she kept an eye out for Barb. She didn't see her anywhere, and her table had been taken by a couple. She gave up looking for Barb and continued to check the pans and wipe down the area as needed before going back to the kitchen. "Any word on your sous-chef position?" Lynette asked.

"The executive chef called me last night. He has someone else in mind with a bachelor's degree and much more experience. But I'm on the list in case it doesn't work out." Claudia shrugged and went back to setting up the coffeepot.

"Maybe something better is out there waiting for you," Lynette said. She felt bad about the flare of relief that Claudia wouldn't be leaving after all.

Claudia nodded. "I was thinking the same thing. I'm not letting it get me down. Something bigger and better is on the horizon."

Lynette appreciated Claudia's positive attitude. It was what had first drawn her to her when they met, and they'd been friends ever since.

"Everything looks pretty good here. I'm going to head home now. I'll be back before the dinner rush." Lynette retrieved her purse and waved to Claudia as she left. She was halfway to her car when she heard the voice she'd been hoping to hear all morning.

"Are you leaving?" Barb called from across the parking lot.

"I am. I'll be back for the dinner buffet." She waited for Barb to catch up to her. "Did you have breakfast?"

"Yeah. I went to the little restaurant down the street. So, are you going home?"

"I am." Lynette hesitated, but she wasn't about to invite Barb to her home. It was her sanctuary.

"Ah. I was hoping we could walk by the river or something."

"I don't usually get a chance to go home in the middle of the day. I'm going to take Starr for a walk. Would you like to join me?" She held her breath waiting for an answer and wondering who'd taken over her voice.

"I'd love to, but I don't want to intrude on your time at home."

Lynette pointed to her car, and Barb followed and climbed into the passenger seat. Exasperation warred with fear as she drove home. What was she thinking? She didn't even really know Barb that well. But she was attractive, and nice, and she wanted to spend time with her. Did that mean she was trustworthy? Maybe, maybe not. She sighed internally. It was too late now. She couldn't exactly drop her off on the side of the road and say she'd changed her mind. But in the future she needed to be more careful. Slipping up could have consequences.

She stayed quiet as she drove the few miles home. Just to be extra careful, she took a more roundabout route, and butterflies fluttered in her stomach when she pulled into her carport. Nobody but Aunt Jen had been to her apartment. She unlocked the door and let Barb go in first, knowing Starr would greet her and she could gauge her response to her.

"She's beautiful." Barb sat on the floor with Starr squirming in her lap.

"Yes. She's my baby." Lynette waited for the questions when Barb stood and picked up Starr's blue Therapy Dog harness, but she placed it back without a word.

"Let's walk first, and then I'm going to make us grilled cheese and tomato soup for lunch."

"Sounds good," Barb answered. "And thank you for letting me intrude on your free time."

Lynette secured Starr's halter and clipped on her leash. "Let's go, sweetie." She chose the one-mile trail, which followed along a river part of the way. She hoped Barb would enjoy it enough so she didn't miss the river walk.

"This is nice." Barb stopped to look at a birch tree on the shore. Starr stopped and sat until she caught up with her and Lynette.

"I think my dog has a new best friend." Lynette grinned. Starr was sensitive to whoever was with her. "She takes care of anyone around her."

Barb chuckled and scratched behind Starr's ear. "She is special. I told you my brother is a Michigan state trooper. He gets to work with service dogs all the time. How long have you had Starr?"

"Seven years. She'll be eight this year." Lynette hugged Starr and absorbed her calm.

"I'm glad you have her. Shall we continue?"

"Yeah." Lynette wrestled with the decision to tell Barb the reason she'd never be without a therapy dog. But there was no reason to. They wouldn't have that kind of friendship.

Lynette relaxed as they continued along the path with easy conversation. Barb pointed out different flora along the way that Lynette had seen but couldn't identify. Starr tugged on her leash as they got close to home. "Here we are." She released Starr, who looked up to make eye contact with her before Lynette nodded, and she galloped to the door.

"Thanks for the walk. It's nice to have someone to share it with," Barb said as she followed Lynette inside.

"Thank you for joining us." Lynette rinsed and refilled Starr's water bowl before washing her hands. She smiled and turned to face Barb. "I know you like Swiss cheese, but I'm going to introduce you to one of the best, and most popular, cheeses in Wisconsin. Grand Cru. It's an Alpine-style cheese, and I love it." She put the sandwiches together and placed them in the pan to cook.

"Sounds perfect. Let me know if I can help with anything." Barb sat at the kitchen table.

Lynette took a deep breath to settle herself and shake off the surreal feeling of having Barb sitting in her kitchen. She'd longed for someone besides her and her aunt to share a meal with at home, and it was happening totally unplanned with Barb. It probably should scare her, but it didn't, and she considered that a positive thing. She remembered a discussion in her recovery group around accepting new friends into your safe space. Fear, distrust, and uncertainty were conferred. None of those fit for her as she stood at her stove with Barb nearby. Maybe some uncertainty, but she'd worked hard in the twelve years since she escaped to learn how to be, and have, friends. This was a perfect way to test how far she'd come in her recovery.

She sat at the table with Barb, and they shared a nice lunch and light conversation. Barb didn't mention Starr's therapy dog harness and didn't push for more personal information. Lynette took the shortest route back to the hotel, feeling a sense of relief and a growing fondness for Barb.

Chapter 9

"Thank you, again for the lunch. I think Grand Cru cheese is my favorite now, too." Barb stretched as she stepped out of Lynette's car. "Will I see you at the dinner buffet tonight?"

"I'll be here," Lynette answered.

"I look forward to it. Take care." It seemed to be getting harder to keep her hands to herself. She'd wanted to wrap her arms around Lynette and pull her close but felt her resistance, and Barb had to respect her feelings. If this attraction turned out to be only one-sided, she'd be disappointed, but it was Lynette's decision, and as disappointing as it would be, she'd accept it.

Barb took the long way back to her room to enjoy the afternoon. She'd enjoyed every minute she'd spent with Lynette and could sense her becoming more relaxed with her. She'd almost asked her about the reason she had a therapy dog, but thought it would be best if Lynette offered the information herself. She hoped she could win her trust enough before it was time for her to go home so that they could see if they could continue to see what might be between them even after she left. She relaxed on her balcony with one of her romance novels until it was time for dinner.

Barb startled awake and blinked to orient herself. She'd been in the middle of a chapter and had fallen asleep. She drank a glass of water before heading to the dinner buffet.

"Hi there." Claudia stepped next to Barb and linked arms with her.

"Hi, Claudia." Barb smiled and leaned away slightly.

"I was hoping I'd get to see you again. How much longer will you be here?" Claudia asked.

Barb tried to think fast. She liked Claudia, but she hoped to spend the time she had left with Lynette. "I'm not sure. Maybe a week or two."

"Cool. I'd like to take you to dinner on the sunset cruise. I'm working tonight, but can you make it tomorrow?" Claudia leaned close and hugged her arm.

Barb could tell Claudia she had tickets for something, but she hated lying. An evening with Claudia wouldn't be as interesting as it would be with Lynette, but she seemed nice enough, and the food was good. Besides, Lynette seemed pretty clear about her boundaries. "Sure. What time tomorrow?"

"I'll pick you up about seven thirty."

"Can I meet you outside the dining area?"

"Sure. Sounds good. I've got work now." Claudia leaned and hugged her before turning to leave.

"One less evening to spend with Lynette," Barb whispered to herself as she returned to the hotel to enjoy the view from her balcony. Her discomfort with Claudia's forwardness triggered thoughts of her own. Did her actions make Lynette uncomfortable? Had she been too pushy with her? *Damn.* The last thing she wanted was to scare her away, and Barb sensed that would be her reaction. She'd have to talk to her tonight.

Barb put her jacket over the chair and hurried to the buffet line. The roasted pork chops smelled delicious, but her focus was on finding Lynette. She filled her plate and lingered at the end of the table hoping to see her. Claudia stepped in front of her as she turned to go back to her table.

"Hey. It's good to see again so soon. Did you get enough of everything?" Claudia leaned and whispered in her ear. "There's more in the kitchen, so if you need anything else, ask." Her breath tickled her neck, and she ran her hand down her back to the waistband of her jeans.

"Uh, thanks, Claudia. Everything smells great. I think I'm good." Barb stepped away and glanced into the kitchen to see Lynette standing in the doorway with a tray in her hands watching them. *Double damn.*

She kept looking to the kitchen as she ate, but Lynette had disappeared. She waited until most of the guests were gone before she went to the kitchen to find her. She found her as she reached the back door. "Lynette, can I talk to you for a minute? Please?"

Lynette stopped and turned toward her. She looked as if she'd been crying, and Barb's stomach dropped.

"Lyn, I need to talk to you."

"It's all right, Barb. I understand. There's nothing to talk about." She started toward her car.

"Lyn, wait." She reached her before she opened her car door. "I wanted to talk to you about something. Can we sit for a minute?"

Lynette slid into the driver's seat and motioned toward the passenger side.

"Thank you." Barb got in and had her attention but wasn't sure how to begin. "I like you. A lot." She took a deep breath and let it out slowly. "I need to know if I've been pushy with you. Like, I don't know, come on too strong?" She tried to put into words what she felt with Claudia. "Like I made you feel uncomfortable. Have I?"

Lynette smiled and reached for her hand. "I like you, too. And I feel things with you, but I wouldn't call them uncomfortable." She looked out the window before she turned in the seat to face her. "I'm not looking for anything romantic. I've been burned before, so my feelings toward you frighten me."

Barb gently stroked Lynette's hand with her thumb. "I never want to scare you or make you uncomfortable. I'm asking you to please tell me if I am."

Lynette looked down at their hands and intertwined their

fingers. "Claudia is my friend and a great person. She's probably a better choice to spend time with than me. She has less... baggage."

"I don't want to spend time with Claudia. I don't mean I dislike her, I mean I want to spend time with you. You're special to me. I feel a connection I'd like to explore."

Lynette sighed deeply and looked conflicted. "I do enjoy spending time with you. But she might be a better choice for you." She gave her a small, sad smile before she drove off, leaving Barb to her thoughts.

Later that evening, Barb relaxed on her balcony with a rare glass of wine. She'd found two bottles of the kind Lynette had ordered on the sunset cruise in a small store near the hotel. She sipped the wine, and her thoughts drifted to Lynette and her words about being burned. Maybe she had a lover who cheated on her or left her. She never understood why people cheated on their lovers. She had no room in her DNA for deceit. Maybe because she fell hard when she found someone she allowed herself to fall for, and had no desire for anyone else. She finished her glass of wine, got ready for bed, and hoped for dreams of Lynette.

Chapter 10

Lynette understood Claudia's interest in Barb, and she certainly couldn't blame her. She really did believe Claudia would be a better choice for Barb. Claudia was fun, and sexual, and she didn't get too attached. She had flings with hotel guests all the time and it never bothered her when they left. Lynette couldn't be that way. She sighed and pulled into her carport. She didn't deny her attraction to Barb, but why she couldn't maintain distance disturbed her. All her concerns melted away when she reached her apartment door and Starr stepped into her open arms. She let her out and fed her before deciding a hot bubble bath was on the agenda. She filled the tub with her favorite scent and wondered if Barb liked bubble baths. She shook the thought away, slipped into the hot water, and felt the tension seep out of her body. Starr lay next to the tub and sat up each time Lynette reached out from under the bubbles. She didn't have all the answers regarding Barb, but at least she could consider her options with a clear mind. She'd worry about protecting her heart later.

She stepped out of the tub and wrapped herself in her oversized warm robe. It was one of her gifts to herself to help dispel memories of stepping out of a seven-minute lukewarm shower and drying off with a towel left over from the previous user. She went to bed warm and relaxed, but her dreams were still fraught with images she wanted to forget.

The next morning, she padded barefoot to the kitchen to make breakfast.

Lynette sprinkled cinnamon on her oatmeal and took the bowl into the living room to watch the morning news. She rarely had the luxury of going to work in late morning. Claudia was covering breakfast alone and she'd cover dinner. Claudia had asked for the change but didn't elaborate on the reason. It didn't matter. Lynette was happy to have the morning off. She was content with her whole flexible work schedule. She rarely had a full day off, but she and Claudia could trade off time as long as the buffet was covered. Starr snuggled on the couch next to her and she attributed her calm to the bubble bath, good night's sleep, and Starr next to her. "Do you think Barb's up yet?" She glanced at the clock. She had three hours to herself before she needed to leave. She sipped her coffee and finished her oatmeal, leaving the last bite for Starr. "Do you think she likes oatmeal?" Her pondering about Barb frustrated her. Her thoughts strayed to her smile, her hazel eyes, her strong body, and the feel of her lips on hers.

"Come on, Starr. Let's go for a walk." Lynette's cell phone rang before she had a chance to hook on her leash.

"Hi, Aunt Jen."

"Hi, honey. I wanted to check in to see how my favorite niece was doing."

"Your only niece is doing fine. I have the morning off today, and I was going to take Starr for a walk."

"I won't keep you long. I wanted to tell you I got a call from a woman who claimed to be a friend of yours. She wanted to make plans to see you but couldn't find your phone number."

Lynette clenched her teeth and her stomach roiled. "Did she give you her name?"

"No. I told her you'd moved to Corpus Christi, Texas, and we'd lost touch. Do you have any idea who she was?"

"No. Did she say how she got your number?"

"I'm sorry, honey, I didn't even think to ask. I'll change it as soon as we hang up."

"Good idea. I'll change mine again, too, and I'll come down to see you and get your new number."

"Maybe it'd be better if we met somewhere in between. Just in case the quiet has been disturbed." The thought of her someone looking for her made her want to be sick. "That sounds safer. How about the Crossroads? I can be there tomorrow at eight a.m."

"Perfect. I'll meet you there and we'll exchange numbers. And don't worry, honey. I can't believe they care about you after so many years."

"I hope you're right. I can't believe he'd come for me after so long. I suppose he could have killed everyone else off, and he's still alive." Her thoughts bounced around in her head making her dizzy. "It was a female who called, right?"

"Yes. I didn't recognize her voice. It wasn't your mother."

"Huh. I'll see you tomorrow, and thanks, Aunt Jen." She sat with her hands shaking as she considered the situation. She'd been so careful over the years, but part of her had always wondered if they'd catch up to her again.

"Come on, Starr. I need to clear my head." She checked the time before tugging Starr out the door and rushing along the trail. She stopped twenty minutes into the walk to catch her breath, and Starr glued herself to her side. "I guess I'll slow down, girl. In fact, let's sit for a minute." Lynette settled on a fallen log and hugged Starr to her chest. "I like our little apartment and being so close to this park. I've already moved three times, and I'm tired of jumping at shadows and living in fear." She hugged Starr tighter. "At least I have you to keep me grounded and sane. I'll stay vigilant and change my phone tomorrow. Let's get home." She continued the walk at a slower pace and arrived home in time to shower and dress for work. She checked the time again before she left to be sure she had time to buy a new phone.

Lynette took a moment to settle herself when she arrived at work.

"Hi," Claudia said.

"Hi. It looks like you have the breakfast dishes taken care of. Shall I start the heating pans for lunch?"

"Sounds good. I'm glad you're here," Claudia said.

Lynette busied herself preparing the lunch buffet and almost managed to push aside her fear. She'd finished filling the pans when Barb arrived.

"Hey there. I missed you this morning." Barb speared a slice of ham as she spoke.

"I'm working late tonight, so Claudia asked me to come in later. Did you sleep well?"

"I did. I'll say it again, I'm glad I chose the room I did. It's quiet there."

"Can we talk later? I've got to get back to the kitchen."

"I look forward to it. I'll be at my table." Barb grinned.

"Ready for me to take out the green beans?" Lynette asked when she returned to the kitchen.

"Yes. Thanks." Claudia removed her apron and left.

Lynette watched her hurry to Barb's table and run her hand over her shoulder and down her arm before she sat across from her. A growl rose unbidden from her belly. She attributed the reaction to her concern after talking to her aunt. She definitely didn't have the room in her life for things like dating. Especially after Aunt Jen's phone call. She went to work washing dishes and refilling pans.

"Hey, Claudia." Lynette didn't want to hold hard feelings for her friend, so she forced herself to smile when Claudia came back into the kitchen.

"Hey. Can I talk to you for a minute?"

"Sure." Lynette dried her hands and followed Claudia to the back room.

"I'm going out with Barb tonight. The other day you told me you were just friends, so I asked her to go to the dinner cruise with me." Claudia paused and looked like she was searching for words. "Barb indicated you two might be closer than friends, so I want to be sure you're okay with this."

Lynette appreciated Claudia's candor. "Barb and I have spent time together, but we're just friends. You know my history. I'm not ready to trust enough for anything more right now. You two go and have a great time. I know the food is fabulous."

"Thanks. See you tomorrow." She hugged her and hurried out the door.

Lynette finished cleaning after the dinner buffet and headed home.

Lynette stepped into her apartment and slid to the floor, holding Starr close. "I'm scared, sweetie. Someone called Aunt Jen. I can't go back there." She buried her face in Starr's fur and let the tears flow. Would life ever be better?

Chapter 11

"This is nice. Thanks for accepting my invitation." Claudia squeezed Barb's hand as she spoke.

"Thanks for inviting me. I love this surf and turf." Barb had to admit Claudia was a pleasant date. She still would've preferred being with Lynette, but Claudia was intelligent and had a great sense of humor and was nice looking. She didn't have Lynette's lovely blue eyes or her soft hair, but still, she was attractive.

"I told Lynette we were going out tonight," Claudia said. "I got the impression you two might be more than friends, but she assured me that wasn't the case. I hope we can see each other again while you're here."

Barb swallowed her bite of lobster and took a sip of water to give herself a moment to think. She wasn't one to give up and if Lynette was willing, she'd keep seeing her until she told her to leave her alone. But she'd told Claudia there was only friendship between them. She had to accept it. "I've only been here a week. I enjoy Lynette's company, and I enjoy yours. I hope that's enough for now." She took another bite of food.

"Sounds good to me. I'm planning on a career as a chef, and I applied for a sous-chef job that went to someone else, so I'm going back to school for a bachelor's degree. It probably won't leave much time for dating."

"That's great. Good luck. Lynette told me you were talented, and I can attest to your prowess in the dessert department. Your cheesecake was wonderful."

"Thanks. I do love to create fancy desserts."

Barb relaxed and enjoyed their easy conversation as they finished the meal and took a stroll along the river after the boat docked. "Thanks again for the lovely evening." Barb walked Claudia to her car and opened the driver's door for her.

"Thank you for agreeing to join me. I'll probably see you in the morning for breakfast." Claudia leaned and placed a quick kiss on her lips, then took her hand, squeezed, and released it before getting in and starting her car.

"See you tomorrow. Good night, Claudia." Barb smiled to let her know the soft kiss was all right. "Sleep well."

Barb reflected on her evening with Claudia as she walked back to the hotel. She'd enjoyed their conversation, and she certainly was hot. She suspected Claudia would have agreed to share an intimate night, but Barb wasn't interested in a roll in the hay. She'd been ribbed by friends for refusing to enjoy a sexual relationship just for the sake of an evening not spent alone. She wanted, *needed*, deeper feelings than lust to share that vulnerability, and she wasn't going to compromise. She thought she'd found it once with her first lover, but she was naïve and believed just because she felt she'd found love, Ann had, too, but Ann chose to move on. She could live vicariously through her romance novels until she found who she was looking for. She stopped for a few minutes to breathe in the night air and watch the river before heading to her room.

She tossed and turned for an hour before falling into a dreamless sleep and woke to the sunshine filtering into her room.

Barb showered and dressed before hurrying to the dining area to look for Lynette. She arrived before the serving pans were out of the kitchen, so she poured herself a cup of coffee and waited by the omelet station.

"Good morning, Barb. It's nice to see you first thing this

morning." Claudia readied the omelet area. "You ready for an omelet?"

"Yes. With Grand Cru cheese, please."

"Ooh. Good choice."

"Is Lynette here this morning?" Barb asked.

"She called in earlier. She said she had some personal business to take care of, and she'd be in for the dinner buffet."

Barb settled at her table and watched the people outside enjoy the beautiful day. She'd hoped to connect with Lynette and maybe go for a walk by the river, and she wanted to check out the downtown and pick up a couple of souvenirs for her family. She finished her breakfast and checked her phone for a missed call before heading to her room. She put a blank SD card in her camera and slipped on her hiking shoes and headed out for an excursion. She reached the area with the small restaurant where she'd had breakfast and stopped in the gift shop next door. It surprised her that her first thought was that Lynette would probably like the small plate with a picture of Grand Cru cheese. She decided to buy it for her and picked up another one to send to her parents. It was a perfect souvenir from Wisconsin. She wandered through the store for a few more minutes, paid for her choices, and left. She settled on one of the benches located on the sidewalk and watched the people for a while before heading to hike along the river. The trees hung over the water as if reaching for a drink, and Barb snapped several pictures of them as well as the water. She breathed in the fresh air and enjoyed mentally cataloging the various trees growing along the riverside. This was a vacation, after all, and sitting in her room pining for someone made no sense. She wandered and snapped photos and raised her face to the sun, loving the freedom and ease filling her soul. Still, she checked her phone for any messages before heading back to the hotel.

"Hey, Barb. I looked for you at lunch." Claudia spoke from the door to the kitchen.

"I've been exploring, and I had a fabulous sandwich in town."

"I bet I know the place. They're well-known in town. I've got to get the dinner menu started. I'm glad you're back." Claudia hurried into the kitchen.

Barb returned to her room and checked her phone for any messages. She'd managed to have a nice afternoon and only think of Lynette a few times. She hoped that Lynette might have thought of her also, but she had a growing uncertainty about that likelihood. She took a quick shower and changed before going downstairs to claim her table for dinner.

"Hi there." Claudia carried two pieces of cheesecake and two forks. "Can I offer you one of my creations?" She set them on the table and sat across from Barb.

"Thanks. Dessert before dinner is never a bad idea, in my opinion." Barb took a bite. "Mmm, great. The hotel is lucky to have you in the kitchen." She swallowed some coffee and took another bite. "Have you heard from Lynette yet?"

"Nothing since she called earlier. Why?" Claudia looked concerned.

"I guess we'll see her tonight, and I suppose it's none of my business where she is." Barb laughed. "We are a couple of busybodies, aren't we?" She felt the pressure in her chest release when Claudia laughed with her.

"I know I said I'm going to be too busy for dating, and you'll be going home eventually, but would you be interested in some company tonight? I don't have anyone at home waiting for me, so I think we could spend some excellent quality time together. No strings." She stroked the top of Barb's hand.

Barb scrambled for an answer, not wanting to hurt Claudia, but honest was the only way she knew how to be. "You're beautiful and sexy, and I'm certainly not a virgin, but I'm holding out for love and happily ever after." She took Claudia's hand and squeezed gently. "I'm sorry. I'm all about the strings."

Claudia sat back in her chair and smiled. "I had to try. Let me know if you change your mind. I'll be in the kitchen. Thanks for sharing pre-dinner dessert with me. I'll admit it was a ruse to spend time with you again." Claudia winked and took their empty plates with her.

Barb sat for a few minutes people-watching out the window and finishing her coffee while allowing thoughts of her time spent with Lynette to flow. She'd enjoyed the time they'd shared together so far and hoped to see more of her. Lynette said she wasn't looking for a romantic relationship, and she could accept that, but she hoped they could have time together as friends at least. Part of her wished she could allow herself to accept Claudia's offer, but she knew she wouldn't feel right about it. She waved to Claudia as she passed the kitchen door on her way out. She wanted to review the brochures she'd collected and plan an outing for the next day. She propped herself up with pillows on the bed, stretched out her legs, and took a deep breath and released it slowly. She'd heard friends and family talk about the restorative powers of a getaway vacation, and now she understood what they meant. Growing up in a military family had instilled in her a sense of protect and serve, and she took pride in her ability to do her job well. She looked forward to returning home, but she recognized the time to herself in a different environment, doing what she wanted, when she wanted, as a necessary respite.

She reviewed her options and turned on the TV just to see what Wisconsin's news looked like.

Chapter 12

Lynette looked in all directions before she parked her car on the side street. She sat long enough to make sure no one was around but not long enough to draw attention. She stepped out of her car pretending to look at a map, but really she was scanning her surroundings for anything that seemed unusual. She walked to the intersection, looked at the map, and checked the road for her aunt's car. She saw her pull up to the curb next to her, and Lynette didn't have to pretend the show of relief. She raised the map and pointed as if showing the driver where she needed to go. Her aunt waved her into the passenger seat, and they made a big show of pointing to the map and waving out the window to show directions. They put their heads down to look like they were reading the map before they spoke.

"Here's my new phone number." Her aunt passed her a note that Lynette slipped into the front pocket of her jeans.

"Here's mine." Lynette passed a note to her aunt, who put it into her own front pocket. "I'm so sorry for this, Aunt Jen. I hope we don't hear anything more."

"I want you to feel safe. I doubt we needed to go through all this tomfoolery, but I want you to be safe, too. I'm sorry your parents got you involved in all this. It wasn't fair, and I'll never forgive my sister for it."

"It happened, but I'm free now. I'd sure like to know who it was that called you, but if it was anyone from the cult, I'm certain it wasn't Mom. She and Dad were completely enmeshed with Matthew and his inner group. She probably never even knew I'd escaped unless he told her. She wouldn't care one way or the other. I do worry, since she's the only one who had your number, that she's involved somehow. Assuming they're all still alive. I think meeting here, where we stopped for gas when you came to save me, was a perfect spot for today. I haven't been back here since," Lynette said.

"No. I haven't either, and that's fine with me. We better get going. I hope you feel more settled by doing this, honey. I'd drive anywhere you needed me to achieve that."

"It might be unnecessary and ridiculous, but it does. Thanks again, Aunt Jen. I hate the thought of moving again, but I might consider it. I can't imagine why anyone would be looking for me."

"You're always welcome to come back to live with me."

"I know I can always count on you. I hope you know how much I appreciate it. I love you." Lynette hugged her aunt and climbed out of her car. She waved and raised the map as if thanking a stranger for her help with directions before driving away.

She stopped on her way home for gasoline and a much-needed break. Visiting the route where her aunt had intervened and where she'd finally found freedom shook her to her core. She'd never forget the oppression of the group and her lingering fear of being hunted down and returned to be subjected to their retribution. She filled her gas tank and drove away as fast as possible. She felt her pocket for her aunt's note several times on her drive home and planned to put it into her new phone as soon as she was safely inside her apartment. She relaxed when she pulled into her carport.

"I'm home, Starr." She absorbed the serenity of her warm body when Starr snuggled into her arms and followed her out the door. She stood leaning against her leg until Lynette encouraged her to go potty. "Go ahead, sweetie. I'm glad to be home, girl. I met Aunt Jen today." Starr's ears perked up at the sound of Jen's name. "We'll go see her soon. Her birthday's coming up." She updated her contacts in her new phone and smiled when she put in Barb's number. She might never use it, but for some reason it was nice to have it there. She ate a cheese sandwich and sipped a cup of hot chocolate before she rested her head back on the couch, and she wished she'd taken the whole day off. Living this way could be exhausting, and she was so very tired of it.

She finished her hot chocolate and fed Starr before leaving for work.

"Hi, Claudia." Lynette put away her purse and joined Claudia in the kitchen.

"Hi there. Glad you're back." She stopped what she was doing and hugged Lynette.

"Thanks. I have a new phone number, and I sent it to your phone this morning."

"Everything okay?"

"Everything's fine. I feel safer changing it once in a while. You know why."

"I do, and I'm glad you're taking care of yourself." Claudia hugged her again and turned to the stove.

"The chicken smells great. Shall I get the carrots ready?"

"Yeah. Thanks, and the mashed potatoes are about ready. Oh, Lynette?"

"Yes?"

"You might want to let Barb know you're back. She was worried, which is sweet since you don't really know her that well."

"Thanks. I will." Lynette turned and asked the question she wasn't sure she wanted an answer to. "How was your date last night?"

Claudia stopped working and turned to face her. "It was nice. I think we're going to be friends, but that's all. I like her, but I'm going to go back to school for my bachelor's degree and I doubt I'll have time to pursue anything more with her. Besides, she'll be going home in a couple of weeks."

"That's great. You didn't tell me you were going for a bachelor's. I think you'll be headed for an executive chef position in no time. I'm glad your date with Barb went well, though." Lynette hid her relief behind a smile. "I'll check her table." She found Barb staring out the window with her hands wrapped around an empty water glass. Lynette's stomach turned knowing she'd been responsible for her furrowed brow. "Hi." She rested her hand on her shoulder so as not to startle her.

Barb's face registered relief and something else. Something that sapped some of the strength from her resolve to keep Barb at a distance. Suddenly, she wanted to grab her and kiss her until she was all Barb felt. She blew out a breath to expel the image and unexpected possessiveness.

Barb stood and pulled her into a quick hug. "I'm so glad you're back."

"Yeah, I'm back. I'm sorry I couldn't contact you earlier." A slight untruth. "But I was with my aunt and—"

"It's okay, Lyn. You don't owe me an explanation. I'm glad you're back."

"I need to help Claudia get the food out, but I wanted to say hello." Lynette turned toward the kitchen.

"Wait." Barb gently took her hand. "Would you have a cup of hot chocolate with me later?"

A tingle of pleasure skittered through Lynette from Barb's intense gaze and tender touch. She needed to nip this in the bud. She needed to say no. "I'll stop by your table after we finish cleaning up." She walked away, leaving Barb grinning ear to ear, and she couldn't deny her satisfaction at knowing it was because of her. She was in big trouble.

Lynette worked steadily the rest of the day, grateful for the distraction from her worries. She'd probably overreacted and her aunt had been safe, but changing phone numbers gave her peace of mind. Her aunt drove through three states to bring her back to the safety of her home, and Lynette's mother was the only one who had her aunt's contact information. So who had called her? And why were they looking for Lynette? She sighed deeply. She didn't want to move again and hoped changing her phone number would be enough. She'd review the caller's conversation with her aunt when she saw her for her birthday.

She finished filling pans and wiped down the surrounding area before heading to the kitchen. "I think we're all set out there." She tossed the soiled towels in a bin and grabbed a couple clean ones.

"Great. I'm finishing the desserts," Claudia said.

Lynette kept an eye on the buffet and refilled the pans when needed while she stole glances at Barb.

"Is everything good out there?" Claudia asked.

"Yep. All good. I have a question for you. My aunt's birthday is coming up, and I'd like to ask you to make a special cake for her."

"I'd love to. What's her favorite?" Claudia looked thrilled.

"Chocolate-banana with that frosting that's not too sweet."

"Interesting combination. It sounds great. I look forward to creating it. When do you need it?"

"Her birthday's next Thursday. I'd also like to invite you to the celebration. Not a big party. Just cake and ice cream and coffee."

"I'd love to join you. Let me know what time."

"Thank you. Let me know how much I owe you for it."

"No way! You're giving me an opportunity to practice my skills and come up with a new recipe. We'll take pictures when you give it to her." Claudia grinned and went back to cooking.

Lynette looked forward to the plans for her aunt. It was the least she could do to pay her back for her help. She was more of a mother to her than her own mother had ever been.

Chapter 13

"Is the offer still good?" Lynette sat across from Barb at her table.

"Absolutely." Barb sat back in her chair, content to watch Lynette enjoy her hot chocolate. "Would you like to take a walk with me along the river?"

Lynette looked at her watch. "I could use a walk." She finished her hot chocolate and stood.

Barb swallowed her last bite of food and followed Lynette out the door.

"This was a good idea." Lynette leaned her forearms on the railing to watch the river flow. "I needed to unwind." She took a deep breath.

"I find it peaceful this time of evening. The crowds seem to disperse, maybe for a late dinner or something. I don't know. I found it like this twice now." Barb watched Lynette enjoy the tranquil scene. She seemed unsettled. Almost scared. "Is everything okay with you tonight?"

"Yes. I'm a little tired. I had a family thing this morning. I'll probably head home soon to relax."

"Ah. Your aunt." Barb hoped Lynette would open up for her, but she wouldn't push. "My aunt and uncle live in California, so I don't see them often. They're both teachers out there and don't travel much. I always thought it would be interesting to go visit the state."

"My aunt lives about forty-five minutes away." Lynette didn't elaborate.

"You said you're from Idaho. Is she also from Idaho? Are you two close?" Barb wanted to keep Lynette near, but she looked exhausted.

"She's like a mother to me, and she's lived in Wisconsin for forty years." Lynette turned and smiled. "I'm pretty tired. Thanks for the walk. It helped me relax."

Barb could tell Lynette had something weighing heavily on her mind but couldn't figure out how to help her. "Relaxing is good. I think I'm finally realizing the value of a vacation myself. I'll walk you to your car."

"I'm glad you're learning to relax. Is being a conservation officer a stressful job?"

"Usually not, but it can be. I live on an island in upper Michigan with a lot of hunters and fishermen. I'm responsible for making sure they're following the laws. Sometimes I have to issue citations and they don't take it well, but mostly I get to cruise around and make my presence known. It's pretty quiet most of the time, but I could be called for something at any time. Here we are." Barb opened the car door for her after Lynette unlocked it. "Get some rest tonight. I'll see you tomorrow."

"Thanks." Lynette hesitated for a second. "Walking with you helped me unwind tonight."

"Anytime." Barb smiled and stepped away from Lynette's car. She took her time returning to her room after Lynette left. She seemed more closed off and private than ever. Barb hoped she could win her trust, but maybe it wasn't meant to be. She watched the river for a few minutes before getting ready for bed.

Barb awoke to a pleasant breeze wafting through the open window. She rolled over, stretched, and enjoyed the feel of being on her own schedule. The sun began to lighten the room, and she watched it brighten. She'd been away from her work duties for over a week and finally felt herself unwind. She rose to take a shower and relaxed under the hot water for a few minutes to enjoy the novelty of a vacation. No rush and no obligations. She dressed, gathered the various brochures she'd collected, and settled on her balcony with a cup of coffee. Barb hoped Lynette would want to go to a few with her, but she was working. She couldn't expect her to take off whenever she wanted to. As far as she knew, she and Claudia were the only employees working the buffets. She'd booked her room for three weeks, but now she considered extending it another week. It might take that long to get Lynette to open up to her. She hadn't asked her about Starr. Why would she need a therapy dog? Why was her aunt like a mother to her? She had questions, and she admitted her curiosity was driven by her attraction to her. She wanted to know her. Where did she come from? What things did she like to do? She had an aunt and a therapy dog, and she worked in the kitchen of a large hotel. There was a lot more to her than those things, and Barb had good instincts about people. Somehow she knew Lyn was someone she wanted more of. She finished her coffee and headed to the dining area for breakfast.

"Good morning." Barb held her plate out so Lynette could set her omelet on it.

"Good morning. Did you sleep well?"

"Oh yes. It's taken a few days, but I'm finally relaxing and leaving work behind. Can you join me for coffee this morning?"

Lynette looked thoughtful. "Yes. I'd like that. I'll stop at your table when I'm done in the kitchen."

"Sounds good. I'll see you later." She'd eaten her breakfast and had two cups of coffee before she wondered if Lyn had changed her mind. She finished her coffee, noted the now nearly empty room, and decided to leave. She'd hoped she could develop something special with Lynette, but maybe she was letting the romantic in her push for something that wasn't likely, or even feasible. Why was she hoping for more with someone who had so little time and lived far away from Barb's real life? Was that the pull? That it couldn't be more than superficial, even if she was trying to kid herself that it could?

"I thought I'd find you here." Lynette stood next to her and leaned against the railing.

"Hey. I'm glad you found me. I missed you at my table." Barb turned to face her.

"Sorry. I was talking to Claudia and lost track of time." She hesitated and bit her lip before taking a deep breath. "I have something to ask you. My aunt's birthday is coming up, and I'd like to invite you for cake and ice cream. Next Thursday."

"I'd love to. Can I pick something up to bring?"

"No. It's only cake and ice cream. I think she'll be touched to have us over. Claudia's going to make the cake."

"I definitely am in!" Barb grinned. "Shall we walk?" She suppressed the urge to take Lynette's hand.

"Yeah. I enjoyed the walk we took last night. I've got to help Claudia with the lunch soon, but I need a break, and I like being with you." She hesitated again, like she wasn't sure what she wanted to say. "I don't have many friends, and I don't trust easily. But something about you makes me want to get to know you. To let you know me." She smiled softly. "Eventually."

Barb had hoped Lynette would become more comfortable with her and was glad to hear it. She'd invited her to meet her aunt who was like a mother to her.

"Does your aunt live near you?" Barb asked.

"Not far. She's an artist."

"I look forward to meeting her. I'm no artist, but do love to take nature pictures. I love to capture waterfalls and natural snow mounds in the winter. Shall we walk more, or do you need to get back?"

"This is nice. Let's go a little farther." Lynette closed her eyes and took a deep breath.

Barb enjoyed seeing Lynette happy. Probably more than she should. "I'm glad you agreed to join me." She continued along the walkway watching Lynette more than the river. She definitely would extend her vacation an extra week. Sometimes, you just knew something was special, even if you didn't know why. And for Barb, that was definitely the case.

Barb left Lynette at the door of the hotel and went to her room. She hadn't planned anything for the morning except to see Lynette at breakfast, so she double-checked the information on the cave tour and decided to plan it for the next day. She hoped Lynette would go with her, but she'd go with or without her. She sat on her balcony and reviewed all the other options. She took another walk by the river before heading back to the dining area for lunch.

"Hi, Barb." Claudia stood behind one of the lunch serving tables. "Are you enjoying your vacation so far?"

"Definitely. Communing with nature is my favorite thing in the world. I love the area, and tomorrow I'm going to tour the cave."

"I think you'll enjoy it. It's a phenomenal example of nature. I'll talk to you later. I've got muffins to bake."

Barb sat at her usual table and laughed at herself. Even on vacation she was a creature of habit. She had the same food every morning, sat at the same table, took a walk each day. She'd gone on vacation to break things up a little, but here she was, pining after a woman she couldn't have anything permanent with, and trying not to be alone. Somehow, she had to break out of this shell she'd constructed around herself. It was time to grow. And if a real friendship developed with Lyn, then it was a bonus she'd consider a gift. If life was different, if they didn't live in different states, maybe there could be something more between them. But life was what it was, and friendship worked no matter where you lived.

Chapter 14

"Hi, Aunt Jen." Lynette answered her phone and took it to the restroom for privacy. "Everything all right?"

"Yes. Everything's quiet. I wanted to say hello and see how you were doing."

"I'm good. I'm working and enjoying the nice weather we've been having. You haven't had any more calls, have you?"

"No. We probably didn't need to change phone numbers, but I don't regret it."

"I feel better that we did it. I'd feel horrible if someone came after you looking for me." Lynette couldn't be sure anyone from the cult was the caller, or even that anyone was still alive, but the fear of punishment for escaping hadn't left her even after twelve years.

"I'm not worried, honey."

"I'm going to change the subject. I was going to surprise you, but I changed my mind in case you made other plans for your birthday. I'm inviting myself and couple of others over for a little happy birthday dessert. Next Thursday. Does that work for you?"

"It sounds lovely. You come anytime. I'll be home all day."

"Can we make it about six thirty? And do you want to invite any of your own friends?"

"Sounds great. I look forward to meeting your couple of others and I'll see if anyone I know is free."

Lynette laughed. "You take care, and I'll see you on Thursday." She disconnected the call and allowed the peace to wash over her from talking to her aunt. She returned to refilling pans with a smile.

"I made plans with my aunt for six thirty on Thursday. Will that give you enough time?" Lynette asked Claudia as she passed through the kitchen with a pan loaded with chicken.

"Sure. I'll make the cake on Wednesday and put it in the freezer."

Lynette made sure all the pans were full and went to check on Barb. She skidded to a stop, stunned by her eagerness. Despite her attempts to keep Barb at a distance, she looked forward to seeing her. Talking to her. Somehow, Barb had begun to break through her defenses, and the scary part was she liked it. She sat across from Barb. "Hi there."

"Hi. It's good to see you. Are you off for the day?"

"No. I wanted to let you know I made arrangements with my aunt for Thursday at six thirty."

"Ah. The birthday bash. Are you sure I can't bring anything?"

"Nope. She always has plenty of coffee, tea, brandy, wine, water, and soft drinks. So, unless you need something special, we should be good."

"Great. I'm looking forward to it. Do you work all day tomorrow?"

"I'm scheduled to. Why?"

"I'm planning on doing the Cave of the Mounds tour tomorrow. Would you like to come with me?"

"Depends on what time you're going."

"They go every half hour, and the last one is at four, unless you want to go Saturday, when the last one is at five. They last an hour."

"Oh. Can we go on Saturday? I'm off at three." Lynette tried to tamp down her excitement.

"Plan on it." Barb smiled. "We'll leave after you get off work and go get tickets."

"I need to stop home and let Starr out. Can I meet you there?"

"Sure. I'll wait for you there."

"I better get back to help Claudia clean up after dinner. See you later." Lynette couldn't squelch her anticipation of their outing. She'd wanted to go on the cave tour for a long time but had never made the time to. Going with Barb made it even more of something to look forward to. She loaded the dishwasher and made sure Claudia was finished before leaving.

"See you tomorrow, Claudia." Lynette went to her car, intentionally avoiding Barb. She felt it was rude but necessary. She had to find a way to keep her feelings under control and she sat in her car debating with herself. It scared her how easy Barb was to talk to, to be with. She rested her head back on the seat and decided she was being silly. She could always say no to Barb. She chuckled at the absurdity of that. She'd scared herself with her enthusiastic response to her invitation to go to the cave. But maybe it was okay to let someone in. Like she'd thought before, Barb would be leaving soon anyway. It wasn't like there was any kind of commitment involved, and she was enjoying someone new to spend time with.

She could handle friendship. The cult had taught her all outsiders were evil and untrustworthy. Learning to trust someone after she escaped was a gradual process, and the one she'd chosen early on had proven untrustworthy. She wanted no repeat disappointments, but she wasn't looking for a relationship, just someone to enjoy time with. It was just about keeping things in perspective. She parked her car and hugged Starr when she stepped in the door. She filled Starr's food bowl, made herself a cup of hot chocolate, and waited for Starr to finish outside before they settled on the couch. "I'll be done in a minute, and we'll go to the park." Starr's ears perked up at the sound of the word. "You're predictable and trusting, and I'm grateful I have you." Lynette scratched under Starr's chin. She finished her drink and clipped on Starr's leash. "Let's go, sweetie."

Lynette relaxed as they followed the familiar path. She

found safety in consistency and familiarity. After the chaos of her childhood, routine and therapy were what had gotten her through the transition into the real world. She hoped one day it would also bring her happiness. Her thoughts wandered to who might have called her aunt looking for her. If Brother Matthew had tested the group's loyalty with his spiked communion drink, and they were still alive, it could have been her mother. She'd be the only one who knew about Aunt Jen, but then, Aunt Jen was sure it hadn't been her. Lynette stopped walking and Starr whined and stared at her. *Peter!* She tried to remember how much she'd disclosed to him about her family. She'd been seventeen and he nineteen when they'd been forced to marry. He'd had a girlfriend he'd wanted to marry, but they weren't given a choice. They'd remained friends through the years of their compulsory joining, but she was certain she'd never told him about Aunt Jen. It was her subconscious secret hope for freedom one day. Her therapist had suggested it in one of her sessions, and she recognized it as the truth. The caller had been female, so Peter probably had nothing to do with it.

"Come on, Starr. Let's get home." The dusky evening shadows felt ominous now, and she wanted the security of her home. She went through the short list of members she'd interacted with and didn't remember any with whom she'd shared personal information. She never had much time for anything except a quick daily shower, a review of her daily duties, and her role of caregiver and teacher for the youngsters. By the time they reached her apartment she had exhausted possibilities except her mother. "Do you think I should be sad about my mom being dead?" She looked at Starr, who appeared to be hanging on every word. Lynette let out an emotionless laugh.

She continued on the path home and turned her thoughts to her aunt's birthday celebration. She'd bought her a new pen for her etchings, but she didn't want to make them uncomfortable and give it to her with Barb and Claudia there. She called her after they arrived home.

"Hi, honey. Everything okay?"

"Yeah. I was thinking of you and thought I'd give you a call."

"I'm glad you did. I'm relaxing with a little TV before bed."

"I wanted to know if you'd be home tomorrow morning. About ten? I'm working later but I have something I want to give you."

"I'll be here, honey, but you don't have to give me anything. You come over for a cup of coffee, and I'll be happy."

"Your birthday is coming. Of course I'll give you a gift." Lynette wiped the unwelcome tears away. "I miss you."

"I miss you, too. I'll have hot chocolate ready." She paused. "Are you okay?"

"I'm okay. The memories are just a little intense right now, and that phone call has me a little spooked. But I'll be okay, I promise. I'll go to a meeting if I feel the need to." She stroked Starr and felt better. "I'll see you tomorrow." Lynette disconnected the call and got ready for bed.

Chapter 15

The sun created orange and yellow streaks across the sky as it rose over the horizon. Barb loved the early hours of the day. She watched the sun illuminate the landscape and the shadows of the trees lengthen and disappear. She drank a cup of coffee and showered before heading to the dining room for breakfast. Claudia was at the omelet station. "Good morning. I see you have omelet duty today."

"Morning. Lynette's visiting her aunt this morning. She'll be in later."

Barb had been at the hotel for over a week and finally felt Lynette relaxing with her a little. She looked forward to spending the time on the cave tour with her. Maybe she could talk her into going on a boat tour soon, too. If not, she'd go alone. It looked like a fantastic way to get phenomenal shots of the river's edge.

Barb returned to her room and looked through the brochures she'd laid out on the table. She checked her SD card and left to photograph more of the unique rock formations. The heat of the morning sun warmed her back as she walked to the river. She leaned on the railing to get some shots of the water flowing over rocks in the shallows, and when she stepped back, she felt a warm hand on her shoulder.

"Be careful you don't fall in." Lynette stepped up from behind her.

"Hey. I thought you were coming in later today." Barb checked her watch, surprised it was nearly noon.

"I gave my aunt her birthday present today, and I'm headed to work now."

"I'll walk back with you. I'm glad you found me because I wanted to talk to you." Barb gathered her thoughts as she fell into step with Lynette. "I've been here over a week and have enjoyed the time we've spent together. I'd like to know if you feel the same way because I want to know if you'd go on a boat tour with me one day? As a date, maybe."

Lynette stopped walking and turned to face her. "Things from my past still affect me today." She raised tear-filled eyes. "I'd like to go on a boat tour with you, and do other things, but you need to know I can only offer you friendship. I worry that you might be hoping for more, but I just can't give it. Do you understand?"

Barb could see Lynette struggle, and her instinct was to pull her into her arms and shield her from whatever she was afraid of, but she reached for her hand. "I like you and enjoy spending time with you. I'm not trying to push you into anything. I have a few more weeks off, and I'd like to spend some of that time with you. As friends. If you're willing."

Lynette was silent as they continued to the hotel, and Barb hoped Lynette had felt her sincerity. She'd take friendship with her if that was all she could offer.

Barb settled on her balcony to enjoy the view and a glass of wine. It reminded her of her date with Lynette, and she let out a sad sigh. She'd talked to her after lunch for a few minutes, and Lynette had seemed more settled, but there was no question there was some distance between them. She had at least two more weeks. She'd enjoy Lynette's company whenever she could and continue to make the most of the beautiful area. She finished her wine and took a walk by the river before heading to the dining room for the dinner buffet.

"Don't pass on the dessert. It's Claudia's crème brûlée," Lynette whispered as she passed her carrying a tray of chicken breasts.

Barb filled her plate, set it on her table, and returned for dessert. There were only four plates of her crème brûlée left. She snatched one and noticed the last ones were gone by the time she got back to her table. She didn't see Lynette again while she finished her meal. The idea that Lynette might be avoiding her saddened her.

Claudia surprised her as she was leaving. "Did you get dessert?" She held out a plate wrapped with plastic.

"I did, but I won't turn down an extra one. It's fantastic." Barb appreciated Claudia's thoughtfulness. "Are you done for the day?"

"I am. Lynette will finish the cleaning, and tomorrow's menu is set. I like to walk by the river before I drive home. Would you join me?"

"Lead the way." Barb appreciated the company. She liked Claudia, and the overt sexual overtones were gone, making things much more comfortable. She followed her toward the opposite direction she'd taken earlier. "I haven't been on this side of the hotel yet."

"It's usually not as crowded as the main walkway." Claudia stopped to look at the river. "How do you like your vacation so far?" she asked.

"I love it. I needed to take time to chill out. It's been years since I took a vacation."

"I'm glad you're here. I know Lynette is glad, too."

"I'm not too sure about that. I like her a lot, but she keeps me at arm's length."

Claudia turned to face her. "I probably shouldn't tell you this, but she watches for you. Every morning she looks for you at your table. Sometimes she makes unnecessary trips under the guise of checking the heating pans to see if you're there."

"Huh." Barb hid her pleasure at the news. "What's her story? She told me she had things in her past."

Claudia was silent for a moment. "Her past is hers to tell. All I'll say is she's had it rough. I don't know all the details, but when she first started working here, I could barely get her to talk. She came in, put her head down, and worked nonstop until I or the boss told her she could go home. I've never seen anyone more efficient in the kitchen. She's the reason the hotel never had to hire anyone else for the kitchen staff." Claudia glanced at her watch. "I better get going. See you tomorrow."

"I'll be at breakfast. Thanks for the extra Crème brûlée." Barb processed what Claudia told her as she walked to her room. It sounded as if Lynette had major issues, possibly from childhood. It would explain her comment about food being taken away and her eating so fast. She appreciated Claudia's respect for her privacy and vowed to show Lynette she could be a good friend.

Chapter 16

The dishes were done, the sink cleaned, and the pans all in the industrial dishwasher. Lynette removed her smock and went to the empty dining area. She didn't know why she thought Barb might be there, but something urged her to look. She sighed at herself. A huge part of her wanted to find her and tell her she wanted more than just friendship. But reality set in, and she headed to her car. Lynette concentrated on her driving and ignored thoughts of Barb.

"Hey, sweetie." She'd never tire of Starr's greeting when she got home. She let her outside, made herself a cup of hot chocolate, and wondered what Barb was doing. Probably watching the water from her balcony. She'd never met anyone who enjoyed the peace of flowing water as much as she did. Her thoughts automatically strayed to the desert conditions she'd endured in Idaho. Hot, dry sand during the day and, except for the scurrying of the desert rats, cold, dead silence at night. Their water supply was held in water towers, and severe punishment was the result of wasting a drop. She'd spent hours soaking in her aunt's tub after her escape, and vowed to never live far from water.

Lynette filled Starr's food bowl and sat on her couch to watch the evening news. It triggered another memory of her fascination with TV. Brother Matthew only allowed videos he deemed suitable for his flock. They never revealed the outside world and suppressed individuality while enforcing the cult's ideology.

She'd been one of a few kids who'd had experience with the outside world before being brought to the cult. It hadn't taken long for their previous life to be forgotten and deemed unworthy, flawed, and evil. When she escaped, she'd been blessed to have Aunt Jen on the outside willing to take in a broken, hungry young woman with no money and only the clothes on her back. Most of the survivors in her therapy group weren't so lucky and had to navigate the foreign outside world on their own. She pushed away the memories and stroked Starr's back. "We might go to group tomorrow. I think I need a meeting." She'd joined the recovery group of cult escapees after her aunt reminded her that freedom from it came from dealing with it. She found sharing her experience and hearing others' experiences, even if they were from other kinds of cult groups, validated her feelings. Stories of their cult lives generally paralleled each other in terms of loss of self and detachment from their parents. She'd been out of the cult for twelve years and still hadn't figured out her spirituality, but she sent a thank-you prayer to whatever power had brought her aunt into her life.

"It's bedtime, sweetie." She took Starr out one more time, went to bed, and quickly fell asleep.

Lynette woke to the feel of Starr nestled against her side. She rolled over and hugged her but didn't remember the dream that must have triggered Starr's response. Her memories from the previous night must have generated anxiety dreams. "I'm so grateful for you," she whispered in Starr's ear and cuddled for a few minutes before getting out of bed to shower and dress.

Starr sniffed every inch of the tiny grassy area next to the table where Lynette sat with her coffee beside the apartment building. She struggled to define her feelings for Barb. She seemed to mean more than only friendship, but Lynette couldn't do it unless she told Barb about her past. At least about Peter. Thoughts of him caused anxiety, and she was tired of feeling anxious. She finished her coffee and took Starr for a short walk before work. She took the short route at a fast clip, and by the time they got back home she'd decided she'd accept Barb's friendship and offer hers back. She'd be leaving soon anyway. There was no reason to burden Barb with details of her chaotic life. She settled into her car and headed to work.

The parking lot was full when she pulled into her spot at the hotel, and she hurried to the kitchen to help Claudia prepare.

"Good morning." Barb stood at the entrance to the kitchen.

"Hi there." Lynette couldn't disguise her pleasure at seeing her.

"I'll be at my table if you feel like having a cup of coffee with me." She smiled.

"If I have time, I will."

"Morning." Claudia spoke as she scrambled eggs. "Could you take care of the waffles, please?"

"Sure." Lynette retrieved the premade waffles from the freezer. She took them to the breakfast serving area and checked the area for supplies. She worked until the crowds thinned before looking for Barb. She wasn't at her table, and she squelched the twinge of disappointment. She needed to get herself under control. *Barb is a friend.* She repeated it several times in her mind, and reviewed Claudia's lunch menu before proceeding to the restroom. Barb was waiting in the hall when she finished. "Hi there," she said.

"Hey. I hoped I'd catch you before the lunch rush."

"You weren't at your table when I checked."

"No. I gave it up to a couple who'd been waiting to sit down. It was crowded this morning. Do you have time for a walk?" Barb asked.

"Definitely." Lynette and Barb walked until they reached the same spot at the railing where they'd stood before. "The sound of flowing water always relaxes me."

"Me, too. I think it happens for most people." Barb leaned on the rail. "Are you still looking forward to the cave Saturday?"

"I am. I need to be sure you understand it's not a date. It's two friends enjoying the tour."

Barb turned to face her. "I get it, Lyn. We're friends going cave exploring. It'll be fun. No pressure for anything more."

"Good. Okay, thanks. We're going cave exploring." She grinned and pushed down the bubbling temptation to kiss Barb. That would definitely muddy the waters.

Barb looked at her watch. "Shall we get you back to work?"

"Yes." She looked at her own watch. "Geez, I never lose track of time." Lynette turned and started walking, but Barb stayed. "Are you coming?"

"No. I'll be there later. You go ahead." Barb smiled.

Lynette continued back to work with warring emotions. Her growing feelings for Barb concerned her and a part of her hoped Barb wouldn't give up on her, but she was pretty certain she just had.

Chapter 17

Barb continued to a quaint restaurant where she ordered a cup of coffee and a sandwich. She would miss Lynette at lunch, but she needed time to think. She still wanted to get close to her, but was she too damaged? Too concerned with the past to look to a future of her own creation? Barb took her time finishing her coffee and watched people stroll past the window for a few minutes. Maybe she'd try one of the water parks. She didn't take the first vacation in five years to spend it chasing a woman who wasn't available. Maybe it would be best if she backed off and convinced her heart all Lynette could be was a new friend before she was in too deep. She left a tip and headed back to her room. She reviewed the pamphlet on the water park and dismissed it. She enjoyed the water if she was in a fishing boat, but sliding down a huge slide with screaming children didn't sound appealing. She'd rather hike along the river and take photos of the rocks. Boring to many people, but she loved it. She ignored the idea that Lynette would probably love it, too.

She took her pile of brochures to her table in the dining area and considered her options.

"Hi there. I missed you at lunch." Lynette stopped at Barb's table.

"I went downtown to check things out. I ate at a little place next to the gift shop."

"I know the place. It's good." She leaned close. "Is everything okay? Are we still going to the cave Saturday?"

"Absolutely. I'm looking forward to it." Barb meant it. She liked Lynette and planned to see her while she was in the area, if it went any further than friendship or not. "Are you off after dinner? Can you stop for a cup of hot chocolate?"

"I'd like to. I can't stay long. I have to let Starr out."

"Great. I'll see you later." Barb finished her meal, contemplating the various things in her life and how people were so complicated. She waited for Lynette, still lost in thought.

"Ready?" Lynette asked.

"Yep." She relaxed as they took the long route along the river. "What's in the bag?" Barb pointed to Lynette's hands.

"A couple leftover pieces of chocolate mousse cake." Lynette grinned.

"Oh. Thanks!" Barb walked quickly until they got to the entrance to her side of the building. "Let's take the stairs. It'll counteract the effects of the extra cake." Barb followed Lynette up the four flights, impressed with her physical condition.

Lynette laughed as she pulled out plastic forks and the cake while Barb made a cup of hot chocolate for them both. "I think it'll take more than a few stairs, but it's a good thing neither of us is overweight." Lynette took a bite and swallowed before she set her fork down and turned to face her. "I'm glad you're okay with the friend thing."

Barb leaned back in her chair. "I'm grateful you're able to be honest with me. I never want to push you into anything you're not comfortable with."

"I appreciate it. Some people wouldn't be so understanding."

"You told me you've been burned before and had things in your past. I'm not pressing you, but if you ever feel the need to talk about it, I'm a pretty good listener." Barb didn't expect Lynette to open up to her, but she figured she'd offer anyway.

"I've had two relationships that ended because my lovers

had affairs. That pretty much soured me on ever trying again. I don't have many friends, so I'd like to consider you one." She took a deep breath and smiled.

"I think that sounds perfect. I look forward to a new friend in my life." Barb took her hand and squeezed gently before letting it go. "Shall we check out the cave brochure?" She grabbed the whole pile she'd collected and spread them out on the small table between their chairs.

"It looks great," Lynette said before taking a sip of her hot chocolate. "I'm really looking forward to it."

"Me, too." Barb checked her watch.

"I'm good for a little while yet unless you want me to leave." Lynette grinned.

"No. I'm sorry. I can be overly protective sometimes. You'll let me know when you have to leave."

"I will." Lynette smiled.

"I've only had two relationships also, but there was no infidelity. That would've been really hard for me to get over, too." Barb's heart hurt at her own memories. It must have been very painful for Lynette.

"I've been told that living through life's tough lessons makes us stronger. Whatever that means," she mumbled.

"I'm no expert, but I've come to believe that as long as I stay honest and true to myself, the people who come into my life will accept me for who I am and what I believe, or move on. I know that I can't change anybody or force them to be who I want or need them to be. I can only accept them for who they are, and if they choose to be in my life, consider it a gift and a learning opportunity. Maybe it just boils down to having the ability to take care of ourselves no matter what life throws at us."

"I admire your insight. I hope one day I'll feel that confident." Lynette finished her hot chocolate and stood. "Now, I better get going."

"Thanks for joining me on my balcony. I enjoy your company. I'll walk you to your car."

Barb watched as Lynette pulled out of the parking lot. The evening had taken a positive turn when Lynette opened up to her about her previous lovers. She'd finally disclosed some personal information, and Barb recognized the struggle going on inside Lynette. Winning her trust was going to be a challenge Barb intended to take on. She stopped by the river on her way back to her room and settled in her chair with her latest romance novel to enjoy a world in which life was easy and predictable with a happy ending.

Chapter 18

Light filtered into Lynette's bedroom window, and music from her clock radio blended with Starr's sporadic whimpers. She took a deep breath, expelled it, and wrapped her arms around Starr next to her on the bed. "Hey, you. I need to get up." Lynette released Starr and rose to take a shower. She washed her hair and stood under the hot spray. She leaned against the shower wall and allowed the feelings to surface that she usually worked so hard to suppress. Barb was sweet, gentle, and considerate. So opposite of Donna, who'd been self-centered and controlling. She'd been drawn to Donna because she could be who Donna wanted her to be and avoid the work of figuring herself out. It seemed easy until she realized she was suffocating, and Donna was off looking for others to conquer.

Lynette dressed, took Starr for a quick walk, and grabbed some cheese and an apple to eat on her way to work.

"Good morning." Lynette spoke to Claudia as she quickly put on her smock and began setting up the omelet station.

"Morning. Wait up. You look frazzled." Claudia followed her to the station and stood in her way.

"Sorry, Claudia. I'm fine. Running late this morning." She wiped the table.

"Lynette. You're not late. Take a breath, relax, we're good here."

Lynette looked at the empty dining area and realized she'd

had an anxiety attack. This was the first one she'd had in over two years. She needed a recovery meeting. "Thanks, Claudia. I'm going to a meeting tonight," Lynette whispered.

"Sounds like a good idea. Is there anything I can do?" Claudia spoke quietly.

"No, but thanks for asking. I'll get the omelets this morning."

"You might as well. You've pretty much got them started." Claudia laughed and Lynette joined her.

Routine and consistency. That's what made her feel better, and she had to remember that. She went to her station and fell into the regular pattern, and the anxiety slid to the background.

"Good morning." Barb stood at the station holding her empty plate.

"Good morning. Same omelet?"

"Yes, please."

"Can I stop by your table after the rush is over?"

Barb smiled, nodded, and continued to the bacon line. Lynette watched as she sat at her usual table. She didn't regret her disclosure to her about her previous lovers and she appreciated Barb's response to offer her experience, but talking about her past brought up memories she wanted to squash.

Lynette finished cleaning and found Barb at her usual table cradling her coffee cup and watching the people out the window. "Are you doing okay?"

"I'm fine." Barb reached for her hand and squeezed gently before releasing it.

"We're still going to the cave tomorrow, aren't we?"

"Absolutely. I'm looking forward to it. I hope you are, too."

"I am." Lynette felt most of her tension ease, and she looked forward to spending the time with Barb. She people-watched with her for a few minutes before going back to work.

"What's the dessert tonight?" Lynette asked as she peeked over Claudia's shoulder.

"Banana pudding." Claudia turned to look at Lynette. "You look more settled than earlier."

"I am." Lynette loaded dishes into the dishwasher. It was true.

"She's good for you." Claudia stood watching her.

"What are you talking about? Who's good for me?"

"Barb. You're calmer and smile more after you spend time with her." Claudia grinned. "My suggestion is to keep seeing her."

Lynette stood staring at Claudia and evaluating her feelings like her therapist had taught her. Claudia was right. She felt grounded with Barb. But was it just the notion of having another friend? Or was it something more? Would it last beyond the moment Barb went back to her real life? She finished cleaning up the kitchen and started on the dining area. She double-checked her work, satisfied it was ready for the next morning, and left to get to her group meeting in time. She arrived in time to pour a cup of coffee and look for a seat.

"Hey, Paul." Lynette sat next to the designated leader of the group. When the group started she was one of the newest members. Now she'd been out of the cult the second longest, but she doubted she'd ever feel truly free of the psychological damage it had done. This group helped her know she wasn't alone. Others had made lives for themselves, and she could, too.

She sat quietly waiting until the room filled and everyone took a seat. The routine of it, the knowledge that it was a place of acceptance, relaxed her. She felt her shoulders release and she could breathe freely again. A young woman she'd never met sat across from her. She doubted she was out of her teens, and she recognized the hollow look in her eyes and the rigid posture. So many had endured worse than herself, and she was reminded of how far she'd come and about the reasons she was there. Encouraging new members did as much to help her as it did them. She smiled at the newcomer and was rewarded with a shy smile before the young woman ducked her head.

Paul leaned forward in his chair and rested his forearms on his knees before he spoke. "Welcome, everyone. This group has been meeting for years, and I want to encourage the new people to participate in the discussion as you're able. Nobody has to talk if they don't want to. Relax, listen, and share your experience only if you're comfortable doing so." He sat back in his chair. "I was fortunate enough to find a therapist that works with cult survivors, and I first came to this meeting six months after escaping from one of The Family cults. I've been out for seventeen years, but some days it still feels like yesterday. I have flashbacks and anxiety attacks, but fortunately, I've gotten to a place where I manage my suicidal thoughts. I'm telling all of you this because I'm here to say it does get better. It does get easier. So, if anyone feels like sharing their story or venting, know it's safe here. Anything you say will never leave this room."

Lynette indicated she wished to speak. "My name's Lynette, and I want to confirm for the new people here today what Paul said is true. I was taken to a small religious cult by my parents when I was a kid and spent twelve years under the cult's control until I escaped. Since I've been free, I've made a life for myself, but this week, I considered telling my story to someone other than my therapist and this group. I ended up changing my mind, but the experience threw me into an anxiety attack. I'm using my therapist and this group to help me find the strength to let someone care about me, but it's scary and will take effort. But I think it'll be worth it. My anxiety only lasted a short time. It used to last days. Just know, like Paul said, it does get better."

Chapter 19

Barb waited in line for a table in the full dining room. She left her jacket on the chair to save herself a seat when she saw Claudia in the omelet line. "Hey, Claudia. Do we have something special on the menu today? It's packed in here."

"Nothing special. It's the weather. We're having a beautiful weekend for outdoor activity, so everyone came to enjoy it. The other hotels are full, too." Claudia set Barb's omelet on her plate and turned to the next person in line.

Barb didn't see Lynette anywhere as she filled her plate with other breakfast food. She finished her meal and relaxed with her coffee to enjoy the variety of people in the room. There were more young couples than she'd seen through the week, and several children squirmed in their seats, probably anxious to get to the water park. She finished her coffee and went back to her room. She hoped Lynette hadn't changed her mind about the cave tour, but she planned to go with or without her. She hadn't asked Claudia if she knew where Lynette was. There could be several reasons she wasn't here, and none of them were her business. She'd been enthusiastic about going to the cave with her, though, so she'd presume it was still the case. She took a walk by the river and stopped in the gift shop. She bought a coffee cup with a picture of the riverboat on it for her brother and a postcard to send to her chief. She settled on a bench to people-watch and enjoy the sunshine sparkle off the water. She mused about how boring many folks would consider this. She rarely concerned herself with what other people thought, but she cared about what Lynette thought. She'd grabbed her attention immediately and had become important to her. That had never happened so quickly with anyone before. Lynette would enjoy relaxing here by the river, and it was one of the things that drew Barb to her. She couldn't imagine being with someone who didn't love nature and all its wonder. She sighed, wondering why that thought even materialized. Lynette was a new friend with whom she could share the many things to do while she was here. Maybe they'd talk or text after she went home, although they'd probably eventually lose touch, as was the way with these things. The thought saddened her. She checked her watch and decided she'd have enough time to hike along the river before lunch.

Barb made a mental note to carry her camera whenever she left the hotel as she watched a pair of eagles soar above her and land amongst the rocks. She arrived back at the hotel in time for the lunch buffet.

"Hi, there." Lynette looked rested. "I missed you at breakfast."

"Yeah. I looked for you," Barb said.

"I had what I call storage locker duty. We get canned goods and other supplies in bulk. It's usually my job to put them away, so I spent the morning restocking shelves."

"You look more relaxed today."

"I am. I slept well, and I like the organizing it takes to work on the shelves."

"Are we still on for the cave tour today?" Barb asked.

"Absolutely. I'm looking forward to it. Are you having lunch here?"

"Yes. I was going to claim my table while it's still available. I can't believe how many people are here this weekend. I'll talk to you later." Barb went to her table, placed her jacket on the chair, and headed to get food. She only lingered a few minutes when she was done and gave her table to someone waiting. She waited for Lynette at the door to the kitchen. "Hi there. I wanted to confirm what time we're leaving."

Lynette walked toward her, totally unaware of how sexy she was. "I'm off at three."

"Okay. So the plan is to meet at the cave?" Barb asked.

"Would you like to go home with me?" Lynette blushed and shook her head. "I mean, to take Starr out. Before we go to the caves."

Barb hesitated for a moment, aware that Lynette was letting her in. "Sure. We can ride together to the cave. I'll meet you back here at three." She knew the temperature in the cave was a constant fifty degrees, so she changed into her hiking pants and shoes when she got to her room and set her jacket on the bed. She exchanged the SD card in her camera with a blank one and finished a cup of coffee before she headed back to the dining room.

It wasn't quite three, so she lingered outside the door. The warmth of Lynette's hand on her shoulder created yearning down to her toes. She turned to face her and instinctively rested her hands on her hips but somehow found the strength not to pull her into her arms. Barb watched Lynette's eyes darken, and neither one moved. Barb took a shaky breath and stepped back. She needed to get herself under control. "We should probably get our tickets."

Lynette nodded. "Yeah. That's a good idea with all the people here this weekend, and then we can take care of Starr and come back." She turned and began walking toward the ticket booth, and Barb followed.

The line for tickets was as long as Barb anticipated, and the only tickets left were for the five o'clock tour. She put the tickets in her hiking pants pocket and reflexively took Lynette's hand when they walked to her car. "I'm glad you suggested getting tickets first. They probably would've been sold out later."

"Yeah. We're all set now." Lynette slowly extracted her hand and pulled her car keys out of her pocket.

Lynette was quiet on the ride, and Barb hoped she hadn't scared her. She didn't consider holding hands too aggressive, but Lynette was different than anyone she'd ever dated and definitely wasn't the touchy-feely type. She stepped out of the car when they arrived, followed Lynette into her apartment, and hoped for another opportunity to hold her hand.

Chapter 20

Lynette filled Starr's bowl and leaned on the kitchen counter. She felt Barb standing behind her before she heard her.

"Everything okay? Do you want me to let Starr out?"

"No. I mean yes, everything's okay. And yes, thank you, let Starr out. She won't go anywhere except to pee and rush back to eat." Lynette took a breath and turned to face Barb. She hadn't moved. "So." Lynette turned toward the counter and picked up Starr's bowl before she turned back. "I'll put this down for her and we can go back to the cave."

Barb took the bowl from her hand and reached past her to put it back on the counter. As she set the bowl down she leaned close and pressed her lips to Lynette's.

The softness of Barb's lips and her warm breath on her cheek as she turned her head to kiss her was Lynette's undoing. She wanted this more than she'd ever wanted anything or anyone before, and it had been a very long time since anyone had showed interest in her. She cradled Barb's head and Barb's tongue tickled her lips, and she opened to her, wanting whatever she was offering. She moaned when Barb wrapped her in her arms and pushed against her. Their breasts pressed against each other and her body flushed with desire. She grew wet and pulled back slightly, too close to losing control. She'd given Barb mixed messages by kissing her, and it wasn't fair. She slowly extricated herself from Barb's embrace and took a deep breath.

Barb leaned her forehead against hers, her breathing ragged. "I hope you have no regrets, because that was the best kiss I've ever known."

Lynette smiled at Barb's admission. "Yes, it was for me, too. I'm sorry."

"Whatever do you think you have to be sorry for?"

"I don't want to lead you on. I care about you, but it's not fair of me to get involved, and I'm not looking for a relationship."

Barb nodded slightly. "We can discuss it all some other time. We probably should get going before the tour leaves without us," Barb said.

"Yeah." Lynette made sure Starr was eating and turned on a light in the kitchen. She hated walking into a dark house.

She followed Barb out the door and tried unsuccessfully not to watch her tight ass as she walked. Just because she couldn't touch didn't mean she shouldn't look. The drive to the cave only took a few minutes.

"Looks like we're in time." Lynette spoke as she hurried to the line of people waiting to enter the cave.

"Yeah. I wouldn't have minded being late," Barb mumbled.

"Come on. You've been looking forward to this." Lynette grinned, pleased to have been Barb's distraction. "Oh my." She pointed to the stalactites and stalagmites at the cave entrance. "This is amazing."

"Wow. It's much more impressive than the pictures." Barb wandered off the path and the guide had to call her back.

"You have to follow the rules." Lynette laughed at Barb's grimace, as she struggled to suppress her own desire to touch the beautiful natural creations.

"I'm glad I did this, and I'm glad you came with me," Barb said. "There are thousands of caves in the United States. I've been to Mammoth Cave in Kentucky and we have a few in the Upper Peninsula of Michigan. Lake Superior has several small caves, caverns really, you can get to by kayak. We have ice caves, too. They're formed from icicles hanging over ledges in the winter. This cave is really amazing. I read in the brochure that they discovered it accidentally in 1939 while blasting for limestone. The different shades of brown in the limestone are quite a feat of nature. I love how quiet it is. I'm glad the kids in the group respect the tranquility."

"Thanks for inviting me. I've worked at the hotel for years and never looked into this. It's fantastic." Lynette breathed in the scent of the cool, damp air and gazed at the walls and ceiling while she tried to imagine being one of the explorers who first discovered this place. What did they think it was? Were they scared or curious? Her own reaction fell in between. Her sequestered childhood hadn't prepared her for the outside world, and at this moment tears ran down her face at the grandeur of the place. She felt Barb step close and lightly rest her hand on her lower back.

"You all right?" Barb spoke quietly.

"I've never seen anything like this. It's incredible." Lynette realized she'd stopped walking and people were gathering behind them. "Sorry. We better keep moving." She swiped away the tears and followed the group, cognizant of Barb a step behind her on her right. They reached an area close to the exit but far enough away to still be able to absorb the peacefulness before stepping out into the sunshine. Lynette blinked away her desire to return to the serenity of the cave. She sighed. They had to come back to the real world eventually.

"Can we stop in the gift shop?" she asked when they reached the exit.

"Sure." Barb led the way.

Lynette held up a mug with the riverboat picture. She mentally reviewed her finances for the month knowing she'd already spent her extra on her aunt's birthday gift. She looked at both sides, placed it back on the shelf, and followed Barb to an area with T-shirts.

"This one is for you." Barb held up a shirt with a picture

from inside the cave on the front. She took it to the checkout, paid, and handed the bag to her.

"Thank you." Lynette clutched the bag to her chest. The only gifts she ever received were birthday presents from her aunt. They'd agreed on a date based on what her aunt had remembered of when her mother was pregnant, but her parents had never acknowledged the day she was born. "I love it." She kissed Barb on the cheek. "Come on. I'll give you a ride to the hotel."

"I can walk. It's not far." Barb faced her and pulled her close. "May I kiss you good night?"

Lynette checked the area. They were alone, and considering what had happened earlier in her apartment, it seemed silly to deny herself any more of Barb's kisses. The kiss began slowly, and Lynette quivered with need. She'd been kissed by Ruth in the cult and remembered it felt nice. Kissing Barb ignited a need and craving so strong it hurt. But she was leading Barb on by kissing her, even though her feelings for Barb went beyond casual kissing. She pulled away and felt the withdrawal like a punch to her gut.

"Are you okay?" Barb held her close.

"No. Kissing you makes me forget everything. I want to feel you everywhere." She began to shake from the struggle going on inside her, and Barb hugged her tighter.

"It's okay. We can go as slow as you need." Barb kissed her forehead.

Lynette allowed herself to believe Barb even as her heart revolted.

"Let's get you home." Barb took her hand and led her to her car. "I will take a ride back to the hotel if you're still offering. It's chilly out here now."

Lynette waited for Barb to settle in her seat before turning to face her. "I haven't told you the whole story about my past."

"You don't have to tell me anything more. The past is the past, and I prefer looking at the present and to the future."

Lynette frowned. Only people without a lot of destruction in their past said things like that. "I lose myself kissing you. All I know is your taste, the warmth and softness of your lips, and the feel of your body against mine. The world falls away as insignificant. I'm leading you on, and it's not fair to you, but I don't want to stop."

"Like I said, we'll go as slow as you need. I don't want to stop either, but you're important to me, and I need you to be comfortable. It was only a kiss, Lyn."

Lynette took a deep breath and expelled it. "Yeah. A kiss I'll never forget." She could tell Barb some of it. The whole story would have to wait until she had Starr for support. "I need to tell you at least one important part of my past." She took another deep breath before beginning to speak. "When I was twelve, my parents moved us to a cult. We were all renamed and I became Sarah. I spent the following twelve years under their control. That's where I had my first relationship and betrayal."

"You don't have to say more if it's hard." Barb took one of her hands in hers. The warmth of her touch soothed her.

"No. You need to know this. I escaped when I was twenty-four, but before I was able to get out, they forced me to marry. I'm still legally married, Barb." Lynette swallowed hard to hold back tears. "Now do you see why I can't keep kissing you? It's just not fair."

Barb was silent for a moment. "Now I understand your reluctance. Were there priests or officials in the cult to perform marriage ceremonies?" Barb stroked her knuckles gently with her thumb.

"It was a religious cult. Not all cults are, but the leader was Brother Matthew. He officiated over all the weddings. What difference does it make?"

"I don't know anything about cults, but I'd question whether he had the authority to marry people." Barb looked deep in thought.

The raw space the revelation left in Lynette's soul was too much, and she didn't want to discuss it any further. "It's getting late. I'll take you back to the hotel now." Lynette reluctantly pulled her hand away from Barb's and immediately felt a chill. It was nothing compared to the feeling of loss at the sad smile Barb offered as she stepped out of the car without looking back.

Chapter 21

The clouds obscured the morning sun, and Barb watched the birds soar over the water and trees below her. She considered what Lynette had told her the night before. She was a strong, brave woman to have survived and made a life for herself. Barb pulled out her phone. She looked up cults and read about several. Too much information put her on overload. How could there possibly be ten thousand active cults in America? And if that was the case, why wasn't there more being done about it? She'd wait until Lynette gave her more details, but she hoped what she suspected was true. The cult leader probably had no authority to perform legal marriage ceremonies. Her phone rang as she was putting it away.

"Good morning." Barb shifted her phone to hear her brother better.

"Hi there, lady of leisure. I don't have a lot of information, but I did check on the cults for you."

"Thanks, Brad. What'd you find?" Perfect timing. She hadn't expected him to have time to do research for her when she'd asked, so she appreciated his call.

"There are many cults isolated in remote areas in Idaho. They segregate themselves and rarely mix with the public outside of their compounds, so we don't know much unless a former member comes forward with information. There are a couple of doomsday cults that law enforcement keeps an eye on, but they're hard to pin down. No one involved talks, so you don't get a good sense of what's going on inside, and most who come out just want to get on with their lives and leave that crazy shit behind. I hope that info helps a little."

"It does. Thanks. See you soon."

She retrieved the mug she'd bought and headed to breakfast.

"Morning, Lyn. Did you get some sleep last night?" Barb asked.

"Morning. After a walk with Starr I was able to settle down. I appreciate you listening to me, and I had a great time at the cave." Lynette looked around. "And before and after."

Barb was happy to see her smile. "I had a great time, too. I'm planning to take a boat tour on the river. I'd love for you to go with me, if you can find the time."

Lynette looked conflicted but regarded her for a long moment before she straightened her spine and spoke. "Yes. Yes, I will."

"Great. Is tomorrow good? It's supposed to be a clear day."

"Yeah. Tomorrow's good as far as I know. I'll double-check with Claudia."

"Okay. I also wanted to give you this." She handed Lynette the mug. "It can remind you of our first date."

"Thank you. I love it." Lynette beamed, then looked sad. "You must be okay with my disclosure last night."

"I'm okay with it. I'll respect any decision you make regarding our relationship. I only hope we can spend time together while I'm here." Barb made a mental note to get tickets for the boat tour as she settled at her table.

She sipped her coffee and studied Lynette, impressed with her efficiency. She poured the mixture onto the grill and folded the finished product like the expert she was. Barb wondered if she'd learned her cooking skills during her time in the cult or since she got out. The need to know all of her puzzled her. There was so much she didn't know about her but wished to learn. Lynette had agreed to go on the boat tour with her, and Barb considered it a step in the right direction. She'd be going home in a couple weeks, but maybe she and Lyn could keep in touch. She loved her job and her quiet life on Drummond Island, but she counted on one hand her number of close friends. She could use a new friend in her life. She finished her breakfast and went to check on tickets but didn't know what time Lynette was available, so she called down to the kitchen and asked for her.

"Hi, Barb." Lynette answered on the first ring.

"Hey there. I'm at the ticket office for the boat tours. I'd like to take the two-hour Upper Dells tour. Any time between eight a.m. and seven p.m. What time can you make it?"

"I can get off at four."

"Okay. I'll get the five to seven tickets."

"That sounds good. And don't forget my aunt's birthday Thursday night."

"I'm looking forward to meeting her. I'll talk to you later." Barb disconnected the call and secured their spots on the boat. Two dates in one week. She was making progress.

She checked the SD card in her camera, pleased she had enough room left for another trip to the cave. She changed into her hiking shoes, secured her camera strap on her shoulder, and proceeded toward the Cave of the Mounds. She'd loved the excursion with Lynette, but today she was on a mission to get some good photos. She sighed at the number of people waiting to get tickets and took a place at the end of the line, but within a few minutes she was among the next group to enter. She followed the guide through the cave and took various shots of the formations and water. The guide obliged her several times when she leaned over the handrail to get a close up of something interesting. She engaged him in a conversation on the formation of limestone and sedimentary rocks, and they talked about the possibility of how the cave originated and the probability of compacted seashells. He seemed as awed as she was at nature's evolution over the past million years. She took a picture of the exit and captured the depth of the cave when they reached the end of the tour. Satisfied she had a few good pictures, she headed to the gift shop to find out where she might get prints made.

By the time she returned to the hotel, lunch was over and Lynette was cleaning up. "Hi there. You missed lunch." She smiled and put a turkey sandwich and blueberry muffin on her table.

"Thanks, I'm famished. I went back to the cave to get some photographs. Does your aunt like photos?" Barb took a bite of her sandwich.

"She's an artist. She loves anything artsy," Lynette said.

"Good. Can you sit for a minute?"

Lynette looked back at the tables she'd been cleaning and slid onto the seat across from Barb. "Were you able to get us on the tour boat tomorrow?"

"Yep. We're all set. Do you have time for hot chocolate on the balcony tonight?"

"As soon as I'm done here. I'm curious about what the photo for my aunt is all about."

"You'll see it Thursday." Barb grinned.

Lynette smiled and stood. "Okay. I'm going to see if Claudia needs a hand. It's cheesecake night tonight."

Barb headed to her room by way of the gift shop. "I need to pick this up on Thursday afternoon at the latest," Barb said to the gift shop owner. "It's a birthday gift for a friend."

"No problem. If you pick out a frame now, I'll process your digital photos and you can take it with you right away." The woman smiled.

"Thank you." Barb chose a medium-sized frame that she imagined would fit on a variety of wall sizes, and the neutral color wouldn't detract from the magnificence of the cave scene. She took a longer route back to the hotel for time to reflect on her first two weeks of vacation. She'd definitely enjoyed relaxing without the stress of waiting for a call sending her to chase down drunken boaters or ATVs racing on private property. A huge part of her would have liked to have someone special to share a vacation with, and as her thoughts moved to unavailable Lyn, she recognized a loneliness she'd suppressed by staying busy with work. She shook off the deep thoughts and headed to her room.

"Hello," Lynette called from the doorway.

"Come on in. I'm on the balcony." Barb didn't trust herself not to pull Lynette into her arms and kiss her nonstop at the door, so she'd left it ajar.

"Hey there. I brought cheesecake."

Barb made two cups of hot chocolate and carried them to the balcony table, intentionally keeping distance between her and Lynette. She reminded herself she was a friend. Nothing more.

"Thanks." Lynette sipped her hot chocolate and let out a soft hum. "I love this stuff."

Barb forced away images of Lynette humming beneath her touch. This friend thing was going to be harder than she thought. "So, can I start on the cheesecake?" She reached for the bag and pulled out the two forks and slices of cake. "Thanks for bringing these."

"No problem." Lynette sat quietly looking over the balcony railing. "Was this hotel your first choice for your vacation?"

"It was for my budget. I haven't taken time off in years, so I wanted this to be as relaxing as possible. I love nature and the water, and my brother suggested Dells, so I looked at all the options." Barb took a bite of her cheesecake. "I liked the cabins and lodges right on the water, but they were out of my price range. This one has turned out to be perfect."

"I'm glad." Lynette set her cup aside and picked up her cheesecake.

"Me, too, because of the view, but mostly because I've met you." Barb watched the emotions play across Lynette's face, pleased when a small smile broke through. "Did you start working at the hotel right after you left the cult?"

Lynette set her empty plate on the table and clasped her hands in her lap. "No. I lived with my aunt for years while I went to therapy and learned how to function in the world. It was after I joined a recovery group and listened to other cult survivors tell their stories of how they'd managed to make their way in the outside world that I applied for a job in the kitchen here." She took a sip from her cup. "I commuted from my aunt's for two years before I could get my own place closer. I've moved four times since working here, just for my own peace of mind. I was scared to death the cult would come after me." She turned and took Barb's hand. "It's a journey. One I'm still on and could last a lifetime, I'm afraid. But I'm grateful our paths have crossed." She released her hand and stood. "I better go let Starr out."

Barb walked her to the door and held herself back from leaning in to kiss her good-bye. "Be careful driving. I'll see you tomorrow." She sighed when she closed the door behind her and reminded herself Lynette only wanted friendship. But she'd identified a need in herself during this vacation, and it wasn't one she should ignore any longer. She was lonely, and it was time to do something about that.

Chapter 22

The evening with Barb had been relaxed and easy. Having an easy time alone with someone she was attracted to was a new experience. She'd worked hard in therapy, on learning to value herself and define her feelings. When Barb kissed her, she felt cared for, respected, and wanted. She decided to accept it and hold it in her heart. She often felt as if she were constantly redefining herself. As if the person she'd been as cult Sarah was still inside her. She wanted to be the free Lynette McCarthy, the most authentic version of herself. Free to choose the life she wanted. Free to love someone and be loved for who she was, without always looking over her shoulder or searching the shadows. She stuffed her ruminations away when she approached her carport and checked the area before getting out of her car. She got goose bumps at the feeling of being watched and rubbed at her arms. Surely she was just being silly. She brushed the feeling away. She'd figure things out one day at a time.

"I'm home, sweetie." She laughed at Starr hopping with her front feet in the air, tail wagging, and her body quivering. Coming home to such enthusiasm helped calm her anxiety and gave her focus on something other than her issues. She put her new riverboat cup away and smiled at Barb's thoughtfulness. She was right. It would always remind her of their first date. She worried about her growing feelings for Barb, but she questioned whether she had the strength to resist. She'd told her about Peter, her previous relationships, and the cult, and Barb still wanted to spend time with her, even date her while she was here. "How can I do that?" She spoke as she let Starr out and filled her food bowl before settling on her couch. An answer didn't come but memories did. She hadn't known what it meant when Ruth approached her one night after lights out. But the subsequent days and nights taught her their sexual encounters were natural for her. When Donna had asked her out, she knew what attraction was but hadn't assimilated Sarah and Lynette before jumping into a committed relationship, and at the time it felt like it had nearly broken her. She sighed. At least she was able to have the memories now without crumbling into despair. She let Starr in and got ready for bed. She fell asleep thinking of Barb and hoping for pleasant dreams.

Lynette awoke the next morning at the jiggle of the bed as Starr jumped off. She frowned at the potted plant by the door that had been tipped over, spilling dirt everywhere. She'd always thought it was too heavy for the racoons to flip, but evidently not. She took the time to clean up and grimaced at the feeling of being watched again. She was getting paranoid. No one had called her aunt's house again, and she never saw anyone lurking about. She finished her usual morning routine and headed to work.

"Good morning," Claudia called from her position at one of the ovens.

"Hi, Claudia. What's the special today?" Lynette asked as she put her purse away and put on her apron.

"I'm baking banana bread. What do you think about adding some chocolate chips to the recipe?"

"I'm all for chocolate. Always."

"Okay if you take the omelet station again today?"

"Yep. I'm on it." Lynette proceeded to set up her assigned area while checking out the dining area for Barb. She wasn't at her usual table, but it was still early. She continued to prep for creating omelets.

"Good morning." Barb stood a few feet away smiling.

"Morning." Lynette set aside the pan she was holding. "You're too early for an omelet."

"I know. I wanted to see if you were here yet, just so I could see you smile before a line of other people want your attention. I'll leave you to your job." Barb filled a coffee cup and took it to her table.

Lynette felt Barb's presence as she continued to make omelets. She thought back to the first time she'd met Donna. She'd approached her and pretty much told her she was going to go out with her. Lynette didn't remember ever being asked. Everything was presumed by Donna, and she hadn't known enough to question anything. When she thought of Barb, she smiled. She'd definitely let her know she was interested but never pushed. Barb had sensitivity to her needs and respect for her feelings. Lynette still had plenty to understand about relationships, but with Barb she sensed a tiny measure of trust trickling into her heart. She heated the pan and scrambled eggs as she watched Barb stride toward her.

"Still too early?" Barb asked.

Lynette slid Barb's omelet onto a plate and handed it to her. "There. Now, go sit." She grinned.

"Have a cup of coffee with me after breakfast?" Barb stood holding her plate.

"I'd like that."

Lynette started to watch Barb walk away before she caught herself and turned back to making omelets for the guests in line. She worked steadily until the room began to empty and no new stragglers showed up. She checked her watch and began to clean up her station. She glanced at Barb's table and wished she hadn't. Barb smiled and winked, and she felt her stare explore her body. She turned and rushed to the kitchen.

"You okay?" Claudia asked.

"Yes. I'm fine. Why?" Lynette tried to calm her quivering belly.

"You looked flushed. Why don't you sit for a minute?"

Claudia looked worried and Lynette cringed at her lie. "I'm okay. It's probably from cooking a zillion omelets." She smiled and hoped she looked more settled.

"All right, but take a break if you're done." Claudia turned back to the stove.

"Good idea. I'll be in the dining area if you need me."

"Where else?" Claudia grinned.

Lynette sat across from Barb and set a blueberry muffin in front of her. "To go with your coffee." She relaxed in the chair and realized how natural it felt to do so. She felt no pretense from Barb. She didn't try to impress anyone. She was who she was, and Lynette liked it.

"Thank you. Where's yours?" Barb broke the muffin in half and offered half to her.

"I'm good. I had an omelet, bacon, and an English muffin already." Lynette took a drink of her coffee.

"Yeah, so did I." Barb chuckled.

"I'm looking forward to the boat trip tonight. Is that the brochure?" She looked at the photo and gaped. "This looks fantastic. I can't believe I didn't know about it."

Barb smiled. "I know. I reacted the same way when I saw it. The shores of Lake Superior are spectacular, too, but this is breathtaking. I can't wait to see it up close and photograph it."

"Do you do a lot of photography?" Lynette never had a camera until her aunt gave her a digital one years ago. Maybe now she'd finally figure out how to use it.

"Not a lot, but I do love it. I usually think about capturing images of nature if I can, but I don't carry my camera around with me at work. How about you? Do you have a camera?"

"I do, but I've only used it a few times."

"Cool. Bring it tonight and we'll get some great shots."

Barb's enthusiasm was contagious, and for the first time in her life, Lynette found herself looking forward to taking pictures.

Lynette met Barb outside of the hotel before walking to the boat dock with her. She carried her camera bag over her shoulder and pretended like she'd done it many times before.

"Wow. This is a big boat." Lynette watched the people ahead of them board and take seats on the top deck.

"Are you okay with this? We don't have to go if you don't want to." Barb held her hand as they waited their turn.

"No, it's fine. I don't think I'd like to be crammed inside, but it's open on top." She checked for available seats as they climbed aboard. "Can we sit on the outside over there?" She pointed to a row of seats on the outer edge.

"Looks great." Barb led her through the crowd without letting go of her hand.

"Thanks." Lynette relaxed and didn't resist leaning on Barb for a moment before sitting up and taking in the view. She watched Barb point her camera at the crowd on the boat and noticed the view showed up on a screen. She pulled her camera out of her pocket, pushed the on button, and saw what was in front of her like Barb's had. She held it up and moved it around, stunned at the view. She pushed the button to take a photo and waited. The screen went black, and she was sure she'd broken it until it showed what was in front of her again. She'd look in the camera's handbook when she got home to find out how to retrieve the images. She pretended to know what she was doing and hoped she actually got pictures. She didn't have an instruction manual, however, to figure out what she was doing with Barb.

Chapter 23

Barb watched Lynette fiddle with her camera like she'd never used it before. She saw her glance at her camera and seemed to figure things out. She was smart, and it was obvious she was used to learning on her own. Barb took several more shots of the shoreline as the boat traveled and relaxed to enjoy the ride. She slid her arm behind Lynette, who somewhere along the way leaned into her embrace and didn't move away. She pointed to several rock formations and told Lynette how much they resembled the ones on Lake Superior. She hoped it might encourage her to visit after Barb went home.

Lynette turned toward her to speak and their lips were inches apart. "This is great." She moved away slightly but lowered her eyes to her lips.

"It is." Barb leaned away. There were way too many people on the boat for a public display. She wanted to kiss Lynette in private.

Lynette seemed to realize where they were and sat up and turned to point out a particularly interesting rock formation.

The two-hour tour went by too fast for Barb's liking, but she joined in the lively conversation of the group and agreed it was well worth the fee. "Do you have to get right home, or can you stop for a cup of hot chocolate?" she asked.

Lynette looked at her watch. Starr should be okay for a little while. She surprised Barb by taking her hand as they walked back to the hotel.

"I'm glad you enjoyed tonight. I absolutely loved it." Barb set a cup of hot chocolate next to Lynette.

"I loved it, too. Thank you, again for another fantastic date." She smiled as she sipped her drink.

"My pleasure." Barb set her cup on the table and gave in to her desire to kiss Lynette.

"Oh my," Lynette murmured and set her cup down. "This is a bad idea." She wove her hands in Barb's hair and deepened the kiss.

Barb pulled away, stood, and gently drew Lynette to her to feel her whole body against hers while they kissed.

Lynette stepped away breathing hard. "That feels so right." She stroked Barb's cheek and moved another step away. "I better get home."

"Yeah. Starr will be pacing unless she's sitting with her legs crossed." Barb smiled and gave Lynette a quick final kiss. "I'll walk you to your car."

"You don't have to do that. I know the way." Lynette smiled but held on to her hand and tugged her to the door.

Lynette didn't pull away when she took her hand as they walked, and Lynette surprised Barb again by leaning in for another kiss before getting into her car. Lynette said it was a bad idea to get involved with her, but Barb sensed her conflict. She'd only been here for two weeks, but she felt their strong connection, and she believed Lynette felt it, too. She'd never been with such an intriguing, sweet, reserved woman before. It was endearing and it seemed to bring out every protective instinct she had. What she was going to do with all this when it was time to leave, she had no idea.

Barb got ready for bed and escaped into one of her romance novels for a while before turning out the light and going to sleep.

The next morning, Barb lost herself in the information she'd accessed on cults with her phone. There were several recovery groups, and the stigma and sense of shame many of the escapees encountered seemed unwarranted. It was fascinating on a research level, and deeply sad now that she knew someone who'd gone through it.

"Good morning." Lynette set a blueberry muffin on Barb's table and sat across from her.

"Morning. Thanks for the muffin. I didn't see you earlier."

"You looked like you were concentrating on your phone. I didn't want to interrupt you."

"Yeah, I was doing some research on cults."

Lynette nodded slowly. "I'm not surprised. Cults are usually isolated and mysterious, so most people are unfamiliar with them and curious."

It sounded like she was quoting from literature she'd read. "Does it bother you?"

"What? That you're looking them up?"

"Yeah." Barb watched Lynette closely. She didn't want to upset her.

Lynette stared out the window for a moment before answering. "No. In fact, I'm glad you want to know about them. It was such a huge part of my life and it shaped who I am." Lynette looked away and took a deep breath. "I'd like to tell you about all of it." She looked at her watch. "After lunch on your balcony?" She smiled.

"Sounds perfect. I'll have hot chocolate ready." Barb relaxed and finished her muffin before leaving. The two-hour riverboat tour was great, and now she wanted to try the one-hour tour. She walked to the ticket booth and hesitated. Lynette would love to go with her. She decided she wouldn't mind going twice if Lynette expressed interest in it. She'd always been fine doing things on her own, and now wasn't the time to stop doing so just because she'd met someone interesting. She liked Lynette's company, but she didn't want to miss an opportunity to do something she enjoyed because she didn't want to do it or wasn't available. She'd never given up her independence before, and she wasn't going to start now.

She spent the next hour awed by the beauty of nature. She took many more pictures and planned to pick out several shots to make into framed photos that her parents would love. She checked the time when she returned to her room and began sorting pictures. She worked for an hour and put her camera away before washing her hands and heading to the dining room.

"Hi there." Barb selected a tuna sandwich from the stack.

"Hi. Did you have a nice morning?"

"I did, but I'm looking forward to you joining me after lunch."

"See you later." Lynette smiled and headed to the kitchen.

Barb continued her research over lunch, though much of it turned her stomach, and waited for Lynette. "Ready?' she asked.

"Yes."

Barb resisted taking Lynette's hand as they walked to her room. She wanted Lynette to lead so she never felt like she didn't have a choice. Lynette picked up her cup of hot chocolate and settled on the balcony.

"I'd love to hear about your experiences, but don't feel like you have to tell me." Barb stroked the top of Lynette's hand.

"You've already told me quite a bit."

"All I've told you is that I was there and forced into marriage. There's more. If it starts to bother me, I'll stop. Okay?"

"It's a deal."

"When I first escaped I was terrified, and I didn't want to tell anyone who I was or where I came from. I wouldn't have survived if it hadn't been for my aunt. I spent many days hiding in her house, reading and learning about the real world. And she spent hours teaching me about life. Sometimes I felt like I'd been dropped onto another planet."

"I'm looking forward to meeting her. She sounds like a special lady." Barb sat back and waited for Lynette to continue.

"I was born in a small town in southern Montana. My mom worked at the local grocery part-time, and my dad did whatever he could find. I remember him working in a coal mine for a short time, and he worked on a crew building roads somewhere near Billings. Anyway, we never had much money, but my parents always said God would provide. They were incredibly religious but had no specific religion. They were constantly looking for the right fit, dragging me to one church or another, so when they heard about a revival meeting featuring Brother Matthew, they packed me up, and we spent three days listening to him preach. My parents were ecstatic. They'd finally found the spiritual leader they'd been looking for. For the next two years, three times a week they'd haul me to his meetings. The crowds grew each week, and by the time I was twelve, he had hundreds of followers and had found an abandoned compound in Idaho for our new home. I'd been home-schooled after my mom pulled me out of kindergarten when she found out the teacher was Native American. Mom claimed she was a heathen and couldn't possibly know how to worship God." Lynette let out a bitter laugh and took a sip from her cup.

"Are you okay? You don't have to say more if it's hard."

"No. I'm fine. I hadn't thought of all this for a long time. Once we got to the cult compound, there was a constant shift in authority. I didn't know what was going on, but I remember feeling unsettled. My parents were determined to be as close to Brother Matthew as possible, and I was assigned to the kitchen and to caring for the younger kids. Like I said, I was home-schooled, so I knew how to read and write, and I knew a little history and math. I became the children's teacher and caregiver. I hated it. I wanted, needed, my parents, but they were too busy ingratiating themselves with Brother Matthew to pay any attention to me." Lynette's clasped hands were white in her lap, and her gaze had taken on a faraway, pinched look.

Barb stood and stretched. "I have an idea." She looked at her watch. "Do you have any plans for tonight after work?"

Lynette looked surprised but relieved. "No. Why?"

"How about if I walk you back to the kitchen, and I invite myself over to your place for hot chocolate after work? Then you can finish, but you'll have Starr there with you."

Lynette sat quietly for a moment, took a deep breath and released it before answering. "That sounds good." She stood and took Barb's hand. "Thank you."

Barb used the time it took to walk with Lynette to reflect on all she'd told her so far. Her distress over her past obviously still lingered on the surface, and she clearly needed the support of a friend. She silently pledged to be that friend and not add to Lynette's anxiety.

Chapter 24

Lynette held Barb's hand on the way back to the kitchen. She'd never allowed herself to get close to a woman after Donna, and now she wondered how much she might've missed. Barb's sensitivity and caring belied her mistrust of relationships. She'd convinced herself no one could be trusted, and she'd relied on that belief for most of her adult life. Her feelings for Barb scared her, and she had no idea how to handle the unspoken understanding between them. She pushed more thoughts aside and enjoyed the beautiful day. The blue sky and sun reminded her how much she had to be grateful for. "We have a few minutes. Can we stop by the river before we go inside?"

"Of course." Barb smiled and followed her to the water's edge. "You okay?"

"I am. I appreciate your thoughtfulness. I've told my story before, but it still brings up feelings I've pushed aside. It'll help with Starr there tonight." She placed her hand over Barb's and intertwined their fingers. "I suppose I should get back to work before Claudia comes looking for me." She didn't move away until Barb squeezed her hand.

She walked into the kitchen as Claudia was finishing the chicken soup. "Ooh. It smells good in here," she said.

"The soup's ready. Would you take the urn out for me, please?" Claudia asked.

"Sure." Lynette took out the soup and set out crackers and

utensils. She finished in time for the first group of guests. She worked steadily, but Barb drew her attention every time she passed through the room. She sat quietly eating and looking out the window. Lynette didn't even try to squelch her excitement at the thought of Barb spending the evening with her.

Lynette finished helping Claudia in the kitchen and cleaned the dining area in preparation for the next day before waving goodbye to Claudia and getting her purse from her locker.

"Ready to go?" Barb stood in the doorway. She'd changed into a pair of khaki pants, and her green polo shirt highlighted her hazel eyes. Gorgeous.

Lynette took a breath. "Ready."

"Lead the way." Barb waited in her car to follow her.

Lynette took the shortcut to her apartment. She wanted a few minutes of familiar activities before she began exhuming memories. She let Starr out and filled her food bowl before putting cups of water in the microwave for hot chocolate. Barb looked relaxed seated on her couch. She liked seeing her in her living space, and that scared her more than the memories she was about to unleash. "Hot chocolate will be ready shortly. Can I get you water or anything?"

"I'm good. Can I do anything? You sure are busy in there." Barb grinned.

"I'm procrastinating. Can you tell?" Lynette let Starr in and settled on the couch next to Barb.

"You sit with Starr. I'll get the hot chocolate." Barb returned to the living room with their cups and sat on a chair across from her. "Are you okay with this? You don't have to talk if you don't want to."

"No. I do want to. I think it will be cathartic to tell you my story." She sighed before beginning. "I wasn't sexually abused like a lot of others in cults. I was neglected and grew up without parents, and we were all punished by the withholding of food and water if anyone spoke against the leader. I learned quickly to keep my mouth shut. We all were renamed when we arrived.

I was given the name Sarah." Lynette stroked Starr's back and she rested her head in her lap. "I told you I was twelve when we moved to the compound, but I don't know the exact date I was born. Everyone in the cult celebrated their birthday on Brother Matthew's in April. We had a big celebration with cake every April first."

"I'm sorry to interrupt, but didn't your parents celebrate your birthday before moving to the cult?" Barb asked.

"No. They were busy trying to keep food on the table and feed their need for spiritual nourishment. I was...a distraction. They kept me fed and clothed, but they weren't interested in me beyond that." Lynette took a deep breath, slowly released it, and wound her fingers in Starr's hair. She took a sip of hot chocolate before continuing. "Anyway, as I said, I was assigned to the kitchen and the younger kids. The adults spent most of the day in the 'holy chamber' meditating and listening to Brother Matthew's sermon. When I was sixteen, one of the older girls, maybe seventeen, took a liking to me and began to come into my room at night. At first she held me and it felt wonderful. I'd never had anyone care about me like that. Soon she began touching me. She'd rub my back and shoulders, then move to my waist and lower." Lynette stopped talking and took a drink from her cup. Starr pushed her head into her hand. "She told me she loved me. No one, not even my parents, had ever told me that, and I believed her. The physical relationship grew, and I looked forward to it every night." Lynette began trembling and Starr crawled halfway into her lap. She took another drink and continued. "Her name was Ruth, and we were together for about a year. I noticed she was gaining weight quickly, and she admitted, after four months, she was pregnant with Brother Matthew's baby, and we were through, that she had to concentrate on being a mother now. I was devastated, but she showed me my sexuality. I knew I was a lesbian, although I didn't know the word at the time.

"I floundered after that. I'd finally felt loved and then it was gone. When I turned seventeen, Brother Matthew decided it was time I married so he'd get more children for the cult. He called them 'faith babies,' and they were his to raise as devotees of the true faith. He chose Peter as my husband and he married us in his sacred inner sanctuary." She could still picture Peter's sweet face, and how sad he'd looked when he'd been given the news. "Peter had a girlfriend he wanted to marry, but we weren't allowed to pick our own mates.

"Brother Matthew conducted Sunday worship every week, and for a few weeks before I escaped he alluded to a final communion that would lead to our rebirth. Everyone was so excited. Most everyone, I think. There were whispers here and there, people who weren't certain but didn't want to question him about it. He put something into the grape juice he used for communion, and my mother told me it was holy water. One of the other elders whispered something about rising to our destiny." She took a moment to compose herself. "I've never been as terrified as I was that day, waiting by the door for my chance. I escaped before the offering for that day, so I don't know if it was a real communion, a mass suicide, or if it was like Jim Jones, who pretended a mass suicide to test who was loyal and who he could trust. Until, obviously, he did it for real and killed nine hundred people. I still don't know if my parents are alive or dead."

"Have you thought possibly if they did commit mass suicide, that Peter might be dead? You'd be a widow." Barb had moved to sit next to her on the couch.

"I have. But I don't know for sure. I probably never will." Lynette leaned on Barb and with Starr on the other side, she felt protected. Safe.

"It seems like there would've been something on the news about a mass of bodies found. Did you ever watch for anything like that?"

"I became obsessed with TV when I discovered it at my aunt's, so I rarely missed a news report. But I never heard anything. He called his group Matthew's Faith, and it wasn't very large compared to ones I've heard of. Nothing like the huge worldwide ones, but logically it still would have made the news if there had been a mass suicide of any number. Now do you see why I just can't get more involved with you? They're still out there. There's something else, too. Last week, when I was off all morning, it was because a woman claiming to be my friend called my aunt looking for me. I've lived in fear of someone coming to get me for years, and now that I'm finally beginning to relax a little, this happens."

"You think it might be someone from the cult?" Barb looked concerned.

"I don't have any friends who would be calling my aunt to find me. The people in my recovery group agreed years ago not to exchange numbers. If any of us have an emergency, we can contact the leader of the group for help." She sighed and rubbed her temple. "I just don't know." She rested her head on Barb's shoulder and absorbed the peace being near her brought.

Chapter 25

Barb shifted enough to be able to stretch her legs out in front of her. She blinked away the sleep and gently replaced her lap with a pillow for Lynette's head. Lynette murmured quietly and changed position slightly on the couch where they'd both fallen asleep.

"Come on, Starr," Barb whispered and went to let her outside. The beautiful morning with the sunshine and blue sky completely contrasted with the dark cloud of anger around her at the memories Lyn had shared with her. It seemed unlikely anyone from that cult would care about her after all this time, but she knew very little about cults. All her information about them came from the internet, and they were all different based on the leader and the twisted ethos they were working under. Lynette might have a valid reason for fear. She thought she heard someone talking, but when she turned toward the trees, there was no one there. Starr was looking, too, though, but soon lost interest. Barb relaxed and shook her head. How could someone live normally after going through what Lyn had?

She checked the cupboard above the coffeepot, pleased to see what she needed to make a pot. She let Starr back in and waited for the coffee to brew while she watched the birds flit through the trees. Lyn had a nice location for her apartment. It was easy to see why she'd settled there.

"I smell coffee." Lynette stood in the kitchen doorway looking sleepy, disheveled, and sexy. "Sorry I fell asleep on you."

Barb smiled. "No problem. I nodded off a few minutes after you, and the next thing I knew it was morning."

"Thanks for letting Starr out." Lynette poured herself a cup of coffee and sat at her kitchen table. "Join me?" She pulled out the chair next to her and yawned while running her hand through her hair.

"What time do you have to leave?" Barb asked.

"By seven."

Lynette stood and pulled a box from the cupboard. "You like oatmeal?" she asked as she held it up.

"Oh yeah."

Barb watched Lynette make the oatmeal. Claudia was right. She was efficient in the kitchen. In fact, she was efficient in general. Every move was graceful, and no energy ever seemed wasted. "You doing all right this morning?"

Lynette turned to face her. "I am. I appreciated you being here and listening to me."

"Of course."

Barb reminded herself to wrap the gift she'd gotten for Lynette's aunt. "I'm looking forward to meeting your aunt. You sure I can't I bring anything?"

"No. Claudia's made a cake, and I have ice cream." Lynette set two bowls on the table and refilled their coffee cups.

"Okay. We'll talk more later." Barb finished her oatmeal and stood to leave. "I guess I'll see you at the breakfast I won't need." She grinned and rested her hands on Lynette's hips. She wanted to kiss her, but instead she caressed her cheek with the back of her fingers, happy Lynette leaned into her touch.

Barb stepped outside and tipped her head to feel the sunshine on her face for a moment before walking to her car. She smiled as she drove to the hotel and laughed out loud when she thought about the fact she'd spent the night with Lynette. The feel of her leaned against her, trusting her, meant she was letting her in, and that pleased Barb very much. She parked and went to her room to shower and change for breakfast even though the only hunger she felt was to see Lynette again. She collected all the clothes she'd worn so far and dropped them off at the hotel laundry before taking a seat at her table with a cup of coffee. She watched Lynette make omelets and decided to get in line, even though she wasn't really hungry.

"Hello again," Lynette said.

"I missed you, so I came for an omelet." Barb laughed as Lynette blushed and turned to the next guest. She finished eating, feeling way too full, and lingered until Lynette disappeared to the kitchen. She wrapped a muffin in a napkin and took it back to her room. Giving Lynette some time to breathe was a good idea.

Barb settled on her balcony and called her brother. He answered on the second ring.

"Hi, Brad."

"Hey. You still on vacation?"

"I am and I'd like to ask you one more thing, please. If you have time, would you mind checking on any reports of a mass of bodies found at any of those Idaho cults twelve years ago?"

"I'll check into for you. You sure you're okay?"

"I am. I plan to stop by to see you on my way home. I'll fill you in on details then."

"Okay. Take care."

She tried to relax with one of her novels, but her thoughts kept straying to Lynette and her story. She'd been neglected and on her own most of her life. The two women she'd trusted had betrayed her, and she had no one to talk to. Her aunt must be a special lady to have gone out of her way to be there for Lynette. It seemed a lifetime ago Barb had wanted to know a woman as well as she wanted to know Lynette, and she hoped she'd give her that chance. She allowed her thoughts to stray back to her first love. Ann was a beautiful woman with silky strawberry-blond hair and arresting gray-blue eyes that had immediately captured Barb's attention. Barb grinned at her memory of how tongue-tied she'd become just looking at her. Her head-over-heels love affair had only lasted two years until Ann declared she felt abandoned by Barb because of the hours she spent at work. Then she was gone, and Barb was alone. She'd learned to appreciate the solitude and to develop interests outside of work. She considered something her mother had told her about certain persons coming into our lives for lessons we needed to learn. Maybe that was Ann's role in her life.

She pushed away the memories, took her book to the bed, and lay down to read. As much as she enjoyed having Lynette asleep on her lap, she hadn't slept well, so her intent to read lasted about five minutes before she was sound asleep. She startled awake by the sound of thunder. She rose from the bed and checked the time. She'd slept for a couple hours. She washed her face and watched the sky darken and storm clouds move in. She picked up her camera and took a few shots of the converging fronts causing the clouds to shift like sands on the shore. The rain began as a slow drizzle and built to a crescendo of downpours, and Barb grabbed her jacket and headed to the dining room. Lynette was busy putting away the pans and cleaning up.

"Hey there," Barb said.

"Hi. You missed lunch, but I have a cheese sandwich set aside for you if you want it."

Barb looked at her watch. Three hours until dinnertime. "I'll take it, thanks." She waited outside the kitchen for Lynette to return with the sandwich and a cup of something hot.

"Claudia made one of her special soups today, corn chowder."

"Yum. Thank you. I'm going back to eat this now. Do you have time for a break?"

"I do. Claudia has everything ready to go for dinner. I need to finish loading the dishwasher. I'll be over after that."

Barb was encouraged by Lynette's smile. She rushed back to finish her sandwich and check her supply of hot chocolate. She'd had an utterly relaxing day and yet she was still floppy tired. It was a good feeling, a truly relaxed one, and she reveled in it as she ate.

She finished her meal and cleaned up before getting the hot water and cups ready. The knock on her door came within a few minutes.

"Glad you made it." Barb opened the door and moved so Lynette could walk past her into the room. Lynette turned and stepped into her arms and kissed her.

"I had to do that. You're so sweet to me, and I appreciate it."

Barb suffered a rare insecure moment. Lynette had been taken advantage of first by the cult, and then by two women she'd allowed to get close. Barb wasn't going to be another one, but how to convince Lynette? She lightly kissed her back. "Come out to the balcony. I made us hot chocolate." She carried the cups to the small table. "Here you go." She sat next to her.

"Thanks. I'm a little tired today."

"Me too. I took a nap before lunch. That's why I was late. You're welcome to lie down here for a while. I'll wake you before you need to go back to work."

Lynette took a drink from her cup and set it on the table. "Come on." She grabbed Barb's hand and pulled her to the bed.

Barb froze when they were side by side on the bed. Lynette snaked her arm over Barb and snuggled into her, so Barb pulled her closer and intertwined their fingers. Lynette shifted so her butt pushed into her belly and Barb drew their clasped hands to Lynette's chest and listened to her soft breathing as she drifted into sleep. It was torture of the loveliest kind. Lynette's body fit perfectly against hers, and the soft mound of her breast rested against her arm. Her body reacted in kind and she shivered.

Barb reached for her travel alarm, careful not to disturb Lynette. She wished she'd asked her when she had to be back to work, so she set the alarm for half an hour before she settled into the comfort of Lynette's warmth.

The repetitive dinging drifted into her dreaming exploration of Lynette's firm belly and the smooth skin over her hip. Her fingertips traced the valley between it and her thigh, toward the delicious destination of her wetness, slick with desire. Desire she'd ignited merely with her touch. Barb lay still and smiled as the dream faded under the insistent drum of the clock. She throbbed with longing and it was time to get up. It was her own fault for lying on the bed with Lynette. She could have stayed on the balcony, drank her hot chocolate, and read her book. Now she'd be uncomfortable for hours. She turned off the alarm as Lynette groaned and rolled over.

"Time to get up?" Lynette smiled.

Barb moved away slightly, afraid of what Lynette might see in her eyes. She cleared her throat. "I wasn't sure how long you had, so I set the alarm." She forced herself to lean away instead of pinning Lynette's arms to the bed and... She mentally shook herself and swung her legs over the side of the bed with her back to Lynette.

"Thank you." Lynette hugged her from behind.

"For what?" Barb took a deep breath.

"For giving me time." Lynette kissed her shoulder and climbed out of bed.

Chapter 26

"That's the last pan." Lynette finished loading the dishwasher. "I'll…" She spoke into an empty room as she turned and looked for Claudia. "I guess she had somewhere to be," she whispered to herself. She grabbed her cleaning supplies and headed to the dining area to clean the tables. She started to wipe the first one and glanced at Barb's table, hoping for one of her smiles. She stopped in her tracks when she saw Claudia sitting across from her with her hand on Barb's arm. Why was she touching Barb? Feelings she couldn't quite define took her unawares. It was like the first time she saw Claudia with Barb. Jealousy. She knew the term, and now she knew the emotion that went with it. She scrubbed the table and moved to the next one. She sprayed it with cleanser and used her last rag to scour it, and stomped to the kitchen. She leaned against the wall until her breathing settled. Claudia had told her she and Barb were only friends, so why was she touching her? "This is ridiculous." She forced herself to walk slowly toward the table. Claudia had moved her hand, but she smiled at Barb and Lynette knew how charming her smile could be. "Hey there. I finished loading the dishwasher." She looked at Claudia as she spoke.

Barb looked at her and back at Claudia.

"Great. I put all the food away, so I'm pretty much done for the day. I'll stop in and double-check everything before I leave." Claudia didn't move after speaking.

Lynette finally looked at Barb, and her world settled. Barb had a way of making her feel as if she were the only one she ever wanted to see. Tears welled and she turned away. She couldn't explain her possessive reaction to herself, much less to Barb.

Barb stood and took her hand. "Are you all right?"

"Yeah. I'm fine."

"Claudia was telling me about the cake she made for your aunt. It sounds pretty cool."

"Have a seat." Claudia pulled over a chair from an empty table.

The longer Lynette stayed, the worse she felt about her reaction. Should she apologize or ignore it? Barb and Claudia seemed oblivious, so she tried to relax and looked at Claudia when she spoke. "I peeked at it in the freezer. It's beautiful. Thanks for making it." She still didn't understand her response to seeing them together, but Claudia was a good friend, and she wasn't quite sure what Barb was yet.

"Do you want us to meet here tomorrow and follow you to your aunt's?" Claudia asked.

Lynette thought for a moment. "Are you okay with that, Barb? You can follow me with your car." She hoped Barb would object and want to ride with her.

"Whatever's easiest. I'm good with that plan."

"Okay. We'll meet here and caravan." She'd talk to Barb alone. If she rode with her, there'd be no chance of her going with Claudia. "Good night. I'll see you guys tomorrow," Lynette said as she left the building.

She drove home looking forward to telling Starr about her day and not feeling silly about it at all.

"Hey, Starr. Let's go for a walk." Lynette clipped on her leash and headed for the trail to the park. "How do you feel about Barb?" she asked as they walked. "I like her a lot, but I'm scared. I'm scared because of Ruth and because of Donna. I know. I know she's not them. Barb is kind and gentle and solid." She stopped and sat on a downed tree. "You're not helping, sweetie."

She rested her hand on Starr's back when she sat next to her. "I'm wrong. You're always a help to me." She wrapped her arms around Starr's neck and hugged her. "I want to sleep with her. I want to have sex with her until we're both exhausted." She sighed. "I don't know if that's what she wants, but I think she wouldn't say no." Lynette stood and began the walk home. She didn't have answers, but talking to Starr always helped her figure things out. Figuring out her feelings for Barb, however, was going to take more than one talk with Starr. A twig snapped nearby and she looked up, but there wasn't anyone around. Still, that eerie feeling came over her once again, and with another glance around, she hurried home, making sure the door was locked behind her.

She finished a cup of hot chocolate and watched the evening news on TV before going to bed.

Lynette woke before her alarm and shook off the remnants of a dream she barely remembered. The lingering arousal convinced her that Barb played a starring role. She wanted Barb's touch, but that wouldn't be wise. She was tired of being scared of what she wanted due to a checkered past. And now she had someone who'd called her aunt looking for her, and she couldn't escape the feeling that someone was out there, watching. There was no way she'd involve Barb with that. She rose and went to take a shower. She'd always thought of the shower as a private place she could be alone with her thoughts and feelings. Even in the cult, it was the only privacy she had for seven minutes a day. This morning she allowed herself a short fantasy of Barb since that was all she could ever have.

Barb's fingers started with her head and slid across her shoulders, over her breasts, tickling her nipples, and gliding down her belly to her pussy. She squirted body wash on her hands and followed the flow of water with her hands. She leaned against the wall, closed her eyes, pictured Barb's smile, and glided her fingers around her throbbing clit until it exploded in release. Her legs quivered and tears welled at the disappointment of being alone in her shower. Was this all her life had to offer? Fleeing fantasies and disappointment?

She dried off and settled her libido before getting dressed and making coffee. She took Starr out for a short walk and poured a bowl of cereal. She wanted oatmeal, but it reminded her of Barb sitting at her table sharing a breakfast. It seemed most of her thoughts revolved around Barb now, and she didn't know how to get her out of her head. Or if she wanted to. But what would that mean when Barb's vacation was over and she was alone again?

She finished her cereal at the same time as Starr finished eating and let her out while she gathered her purse and keys. She let her back in and headed to work. And to Barb.

Chapter 27

Shadows crept across the floor in a losing battle with the tendrils of light filtering into the room. Barb checked the time out of habit and turned her attention back to enjoy the early-morning peace. She'd left the balcony door open for fresh air, and the breeze mixed with the early sunshine reminded her of Lynette. Most things did since she'd met her. She'd felt the instant connection when they first met, and it had grown stronger in the days she'd been here. She got up and made herself a cup of coffee to take to the balcony. An unsettled knot formed in her stomach. She sipped her coffee and decided a run would help. She wasn't used to the inactivity and extra food she'd been indulging in. She finished her coffee, changed into a pair of sweatpants, and made a mental note to check on her laundry as she left her room.

The road along the river was nearly empty, and she enjoyed the solitude as she ran. The river flowed next to her as she fell into a rhythm and let her mind empty. She paused when she passed the point where she and Lynette had stopped to talk. Lynette filled her senses. The sparkle in her eyes when she smiled. The intensity in her expression when she spoke of her time in the cult. The softness of her lips when they'd kissed. The feel of her body pressed against hers. She nearly tripped and stopped running when she remembered the feel of her asleep in her arms. Vulnerable. Trusting. She shook off her ruminations and picked up her pace again. She crossed the street to head back to the hotel and passed the gift shop that reminded her of Lynette. She ran past the small restaurant where she'd gotten a sandwich and smiled at how familiar the place had become. She slowed to enjoy the growing heat of the morning sun. A few early risers ambled by, and she walked the rest of the way to the hotel to take a shower and head to breakfast. And Lynette.

Barb took her full plate to her usual table and stole glances at Lynette while she ate. She watched her work for a few minutes and caught her eye when she looked up. The blush that crept up from her neck to her cheeks made Barb want to stroke her cheeks. They'd definitely have to talk later. Barb finished her breakfast and waited until the last person in the omelet line finished before she approached her. "Do you have time for a muffin on the balcony before lunch?"

"I'll make time." Lynette grinned. "I'll be over after I clean up."

"See you there," Barb said. She grabbed a cinnamon and a blueberry muffin on her way back to her room. She filled the coffeemaker with water, and fifteen minutes later, Lynette knocked on the door. "Glad you could make it." She stepped aside to let her in.

"I couldn't pass up coffee on the balcony. It's become our thing, and I look forward to it." She sat and picked up her coffee cup. "I was thinking of something. For tonight."

Barb sat in the other chair and took a bite of muffin. "Okay."

"I haven't talked to Claudia yet, but I thought we could all ride together. I could drive and bring you both back to the hotel afterward. Claudia lives north of here and my aunt is south, and I'm in the middle, so it made sense to me."

"It's up to you, but that's a lot of driving, isn't it?"

"I don't mind, but I'll check with Claudia first."

"Okay, but if Claudia lives north, she could probably drop me off on her way home." Barb realized Lynette didn't like that idea. Her scowl only lasted a few seconds, but it was there. "I'd rather ride with you, though." She watched Lynette's smile spread and knew she'd said the right thing. Lynette left and she went to check on her laundry.

She returned with an armload of clothes and put them away before changing and heading to meet Lynette and Claudia.

"Wow. The cake is beautiful, Claudia." Barb helped Claudia and Lynette load the car. She had her gift wrapped by the hotel clerk and packed it carefully in her backpack. She began to step into the back seat of Lynette's car when Claudia stopped her.

"You get in front. I'll sit in back and keep an eye on the cake," Claudia said.

Barb slid into the front seat and watched Lynette as she drove. She held the steering wheel at ten and two like she remembered from her own driver's education class. She paid close attention to the road and other cars and all traffic lights and never looked away. "Did your aunt teach you to drive? You're a careful driver."

"Yes. Aunt Jen taught me to drive, how to use a cell phone, and what the internet was. I owe her my life."

"I can't wait to meet her. She's got to be a very special lady."

"She is. I'm glad you guys are with me. She'll be thrilled to see that I have friends." Lynette grinned and glanced at Barb quickly before turning her attention back to her driving.

Claudia was quiet in the back seat, and Barb watched the view out the window as they traveled. Lynette's aunt's house was nestled in a group of trees at the end of a paved road, and she waved from the front doorway when they arrived. She was a beautiful woman. Streaks of gray highlighted her brown hair, and her dark eyes sparkled when she smiled. "Welcome." Her sundress flowed around her legs as she walked toward them. She had a willowy figure and was taller than Lynette, as well as bustier. She wrapped her arms around Lynette when she stepped out of the car.

Barb held the bag with ice cream and stood back with

Claudia, who was holding the cake. She smiled when Lynette introduced her aunt as Jennifer Strams. She felt her regard her with the same intensity as Lynette had when they'd first met. "It's nice to meet you." She wasn't sure how to address her.

"Please, call me Jen. I've heard good things about you, Barb. Come on. Let's all go eat cake."

"And ice cream," Lynette said.

Claudia smiled and led the way.

Barb waited for Lynette and followed her into the cozy house. The first thing she noticed was the beautiful oil paintings on the walls. It was a single level two-bedroom, with a laundry room and an all-season room with a gas fireplace. It looked like perfect lighting for the paintings sitting on the easels lining one wall. Barb settled on one of the kitchen chairs and Jen offered drinks while Claudia set the cake in the middle of the table and lit six candles.

"Come on, Aunt Jen. Sit down and blow out your candles," Lynette said. "Should we wait awhile? Are any of your friends coming?" she asked.

"No. I didn't invite anyone. I wanted to have time with just you." She smiled. "Six candles, huh? I have to multiply that by ten!" She chuckled and blew out the candles.

Lynette scooped ice cream, Claudia cut the cake, and Barb engaged Jen in conversation about her art. She set the gift she'd brought on the table in front of her.

"Oh. You didn't have to get me a gift." Jen's smile and enthusiasm wiped away any doubt she'd like it. The photo Barb had taken in the cave highlighted the various formations and the water. Jen immediately hung it on one of the few empty spots on the wall in her living room. She rushed back and drew Barb into a warm hug. "It's perfect. I love it."

She didn't miss the way Lynette looked at her, like she'd done something heroic, and it made her chest swell.

Barb relaxed after finishing the small glass of brandy Jen

insisted they all have to celebrate. It was obvious Claudia knew Jen well, and she squashed the sudden surge of jealousy. Lynette and Claudia had been friends for years. Of course she'd have met her aunt. She focused on the fact that she was there now because Lynette invited her.

Chapter 28

"Thank you for helping me celebrate another birthday, honey," Aunt Jen said. "I like your new friend, Barb, too. I can tell she's taken with you. Does she treat you well?"

"I don't know about all that, but she does treat me well and we've been on a sort of date."

"A date. I'm so glad." Aunt Jen wrapped her in a hug and squeezed her.

"It's not a big deal. We wanted to get to know each other better." Lynette knew her aunt would see through her rationalization.

"Whatever you say." She smirked, then looked serious. "You go as slow as you need to. You deserve to be happy, and if she's the one to make that happen, I'm all for it. You be careful driving and let me know when you get home."

"I will." Lynette waved and went to the car where Barb and Claudia waited for her.

"That was fun." Claudia yawned in the back seat.

"It was," Barb said. "Did you enjoy it, Lyn?"

"I did, but more importantly, Aunt Jen did. She loves a party. Thanks for joining me."

The rest of the ride home was quiet except for the flip-flopping of her belly. Claudia fell asleep and Barb seemed content to ride in silence. Her aunt liked Barb, and she was an excellent judge of character. She trusted her aunt to know about people. Aunt Jen had never trusted Donna and probably wouldn't have trusted Ruth either, if she'd ever met her. Thoughts of Ruth rekindled the fear of her aunt's caller. If she was alive, it certainly could have been her. She glanced quickly at Barb and caught her smiling at her. She felt the heat rise up her neck to her cheeks, and she shifted in her seat.

"That cake was outstanding, Claudia." Barb turned to face her.

"Thanks. I'm glad it turned out so well. We might have to see if the boss will let me make it at work."

"I'll vote for that," Barb said.

"I like that idea, too," said Lynette. "Here we are." She pulled the car into the hotel parking lot and stepped out of her car, glancing around. The staff parking lot was clear except for a couple familiar cars.

"Thanks for driving." Claudia hugged her and Barb, who'd also gotten out of the car. She waved as she drove away.

"You be careful driving home." Barb stepped close and cupped Lynette's face with her hands. They were warm and gentle and Lynette leaned into her touch. "May I kiss you good night?"

Lynette smiled at the request and began to laugh when she thought back to the kisses they already shared. "You better." She wrapped her arms around her waist and pulled her against her.

Barb's sweep of her lips across hers, as light as a feather, sent a blaze of need to her core. Lynette murmured for more and Barb pressed harder and ran her tongue between them. Their kiss lasted long enough for Lynette to forget she wasn't supposed to be doing it. She pushed Barb against the side of the car to feel the total body contact. Barb groaned, and Lynette realized she'd gone too far again. She stepped back, but Barb held her tightly against her.

"You're doing it again." Barb sounded as if she'd run a mile. "It's okay. You're not leading me on or being untruthful." She released her tight hold. "You told me about Peter and Ruth. Peter is back at the cult or maybe dead. Ruth was an idiot to treat you badly. You've been totally honest, and I know what I'm doing. This was a kiss, Lyn. We are not having sex."

Lynette blinked. "You don't want to?" she asked.

"I don't want to have hormone-induced sex with you. If we both decide the time is right, I want to make love to you. There's a big difference to me. Do you understand?"

Lynette didn't understand. Her experiences had been kissing led to bed, led to heartache. End of story. A small twinge of hope began to soften the hardened walls protecting her heart.

Lynette tossed and turned in bed when she got home. Starr never left her side even when she rolled over, and more than once she'd sat up and looked at the window like she'd heard something. But then she'd lain down again, allowing Lynette's pulse to return to normal. Her thoughts raced between Ruth possibly looking for her and Barb's declaration that she didn't want to have sex with her. She didn't think it was a good idea because she felt it was leading Barb on, but she thought she'd at least want to.

She woke to her alarm and took a hot shower and dressed quickly, anxious to talk to Barb. She checked the area around her carport before getting into her car and took note of any cars following her on the way to the hotel.

"Good morning." Barb looked relaxed and sexy in black jeans and a T-shirt with a picture of the Cave of the Mounds on the front. She took her omelet to her table with a coffee.

Lynette quit stealing glances at her, not wanting to make her uncomfortable. She planned to talk to her after breakfast about the previous night. She'd lain awake for hours trying to figure out what she was missing. Why didn't Barb want to go to bed with her? There was something she'd misunderstood. She remembered the meeting her group had devoted to relationships. Many of the members had married outsiders after escaping their cult, and it was difficult for them to separate who they had been in the cult from who they were as a free person. She could relate to that with Donna. It had been too soon for her to try to share who she was with someone. She'd needed time to figure out who that was. Was she there yet? She pushed aside any more heavy thoughts and concentrated on making omelets.

"I have a piece of cake for each of us," Claudia whispered in Lynette's ear. "Meet me at Barb's table in five minutes." She left as quickly as she arrived. So much for a private talk with Barb. She cleaned the area, poured herself a cup of coffee, and went to check out the cake. "I thought we left the cake with Aunt Jen." She pulled a chair from another table to sit.

"I wanted to, but Jen insisted I take back three pieces for us today. I told her we'd celebrate her birthday again for her."

Lynette relaxed and enjoyed the conversation, which mainly revolved around the visit to her aunt's. Claudia finally left to go back to the kitchen.

"Feel like a few minutes on my balcony?" Barb asked.

Lynette stood and followed Barb out.

"Coffee? Or hot chocolate?" Barb asked when they arrived.

"Neither, thanks. I'm full." Lynette watched the river below and the people walking past, oblivious of being watched from on high. "I need to ask you something about what you said last night." She turned to face Barb. "Why don't you want to have sex with me?"

Barb tipped her head and looked at her long enough that Lynette thought she wouldn't answer. "I'm trying to figure out what you're asking. I'd have to be straight *and* stupid to not want to have sex with you. You're a beautiful, sexy, intelligent, strong woman. You've been hurt in the past, and I understand why you're hesitant to get involved again." She looked at her watch. "Do you have time to get into this now?"

"Yes. I need to figure this out."

"Okay. Come on." Barb tugged her to the bed.

"Wait. What are we doing?" Lynette pulled away.

"We can sit outside if you want, but I wanted to hold you when we talk."

Lynette sat on the edge of the bed while Barb got extra pillows from the closet.

"There. Now we can be comfortable, and I can hold your hand. If that's all right with you."

Lynette settled on the bed propped up by the extra pillows. It was pretty comfy with Barb close to her, but she clasped her hands in her lap.

Barb began talking. "I dated a woman during college, and she was the first one I ever slept with. Okay, had sex with. It confirmed my sexual orientation for me, but our relationship didn't last. After I graduated from the conservation officer academy, I met Ann. We had a long-term relationship, and she's the only woman I've ever had a loving relationship with. It ended because she got tired of the hours I had to spend on my job. I've dated a few other women since, but never felt the emotional connection it takes for me to be that vulnerable again. I need more feelings involved than only attraction to be able to jump into bed with someone. Does that answer your question? Believe me, it's not that I don't think about you in the middle of the night."

"I think of you, too." Lynette spoke barely above a whisper. She didn't know what it meant other than she wanted Barb. Her minimal experience told her she wanted to have sex with her. Could it mean she wanted something more substantial? Something more permanent? The thought scared her, but she trusted Barb to be honest with her. "Would you hold me now?"

Barb gathered her in her arms and drew her close.

Chapter 29

The day had been sunny and warm, so Barb wasn't surprised at the mild evening temperature. She stood by the river with her camera and attempted to capture the sparkles of the late-day sun on the water. She would have enjoyed having Lynette's company on her outing, but she'd left for the day after dinner. Barb feared she'd scared her away by explaining her feelings about intimacy. She sighed. Lynette was definitely special to her, and she wanted to spend more time with her. Things were quiet at home when she talked to her chief earlier, and he had assured her she could have another week off. Would one more week be enough time with Lynette? It was strange to be dreading the trip home. She headed back to her room to do some reading before bed.

The knock on the door startled her, and her first thought was of Lynette, but Claudia stood at her door smiling and holding a plate of cookies. "Hi. Would you be my taste tester?"

Barb ushered her into the room. "They smell great. A cup of coffee to go with them?"

"Decaf, please." Claudia took the plate to the balcony. "Wow. I see why Lynette talks so much about this view."

Barb set their coffees on the table and joined Claudia at the railing. "Yeah. I'm glad I chose this room. This is a nice surprise." She reached for a cookie.

"Lynette went to a meeting tonight, so… Oh dear. She did tell you about her meetings, didn't she?" Claudia looked concerned.

"Yes, she did. No worries."

Claudia let out a small sigh of relief. "She left a little early today, and I think these turned out great, but I wanted another opinion."

"They're excellent. You're extremely talented, you know."

"Thanks. I love cooking. Anyway, I wanted to tell you something." Claudia seemed to be collecting her thoughts before she continued. "When Lynette started working with me, I thought she was weird. She was nice enough but had few social skills. I liked her but felt her pushing me away." Claudia took a bite of cookie before continuing. "It took a while, but we became close friends. She told me about the cult and her previous lovers. She was like a kid discovering a new world, and I became protective of her."

"I know she considers you a good friend. I imagine it took time for her to trust you."

"Oh yes, and I would never do anything to jeopardize that trust. So, with that in mind, I'd like to know what your intentions are with her."

Barb smiled slightly at the old fashioned phrasing. "I have no intentions, Claudia. I like her a lot, but I would never take advantage of her or push her into anything she didn't want. I'll be going home in a week or so, and it's tough to keep up a long-distance relationship. I'm taking things a day at a time, just like she told me she does. We talked this morning, and I'm worried I might have scared her away."

"Hmm. You didn't have sex, did you?"

"No. No sex."

"Once Lynette became more comfortable with me, we talked about our sexuality and the fact we were both lesbians. She surprised me by automatically expecting us to have sex. To her, that's what being a lesbian meant. What love means, too. She told me stories of the abuse that went on in the cult. I'm talking statutory rape. Fifteen-year-olds having babies, but thankfully she wasn't one of them."

"Now I understand. It's what we talked about today. She couldn't figure out, the way she put it, why I didn't want to have sex with her. And it's not that I don't want to, but there are bigger things at stake. It's way more complicated than a simple vacation tryst, you know?"

"I know she cares about you, but she's unsure how to proceed. I remember you're all about strings, but I'm here to let you know you'd be in big trouble with me if you hurt her."

"Duly noted." Barb grinned. She had no intention of hurting Lynette but hoped she could protect herself, too. "Believe me when I say I'm thinking everything through."

"I guess I'll head home. Thanks for helping me test the cookies. There'll be a few extra for you and Lynette tomorrow." Claudia stood and hugged her good-bye.

Barb finished her cookie while she watched the sunset. What on earth was she going to do?

She spent an hour reading before shutting off the light and going to sleep.

The dining area was full by the time Barb arrived for breakfast. She'd slept past her usual time without regrets. The dream involved her and Lynette making love on a sailboat in the middle of a calm lake, their naked bodies warmed by the sun. It was no wonder she wanted to linger in the afterglow. She sat at the only available table in the corner.

"Good morning." Lynette's smile eased the tension in her gut.

"Good morning." Barb didn't want to take her omelet and leave, but she didn't want to invade Lynette's privacy by asking about her meeting. "Claudia has cookies for us. Want to share on my balcony after breakfast?" Barb asked.

"I'll be there." Another smile helped ease Barb's uneasiness. Things would be okay. She ate her omelet glancing at Lynette, catching her eye several times. She finished her coffee and took a brisk walk outside on her way to her room. She'd only waited half an hour when she heard the knock at the door.

"Glad you made it." Barb took Lynette's hand and guided her into the room. She surprised her by moving into her arms and kissing her quickly. Barb wanted more kisses, but that was for Lynette to give.

Lynette took her hand and walked to the balcony. "Yum. Claudia's cookies." She grabbed one and took a bite.

"Yep." Barb copied her by picking up a cookie and taking a bite. "Do you want a cup of coffee to go with it?"

"I'm coffee'd out, I think. But thanks."

"Are you doing okay after our talk yesterday morning?"

"I am. I can't say I've figured myself out yet, but I think I'm making progress. I'm sorry if I sort of melted. I'm not used to dealing with feelings, but what I know for sure is I like you, and I like how I feel when I'm with you. That's new for me because I think I'm learning how to feel the important things."

"I sure don't have all the answers, but I know you are the most interesting, sexy, beautiful woman I've ever met, and I want to get to know you and get as close to you as you'll allow me to."

"How much longer are you going to be here? It's been three weeks, hasn't it?"

"I'm going to take another week. I wouldn't mind doing the cave tour again."

"I'd like that, too."

"I don't mean to be nosy, but did you talk to your aunt about who called looking for you?"

"No. It was her birthday celebration, and I didn't want to make it about anything else. I'll ask her the next time I talk to her. Aunt Jen has lived in her house for forty years. She refuses to move, and she shouldn't have to, but my mother, if she's still alive, knows where she lives. It worries me sometimes." She shook her head and set the half-eaten cookie down. "Lately I'm jumping at shadows, convinced there's someone watching me. I know it's irrational, but I can't seem to help it."

"What if your mom isn't dead? Would she try to contact you?"

"I can't imagine why," Lynette said. "She didn't give two hoots about me then. I doubt she'd want me now. I think Aunt Jen would have recognized her voice, if she'd called. I do worry if she's still alive that she may have given my aunt's number to someone. Maybe Ruth." Lynette rested her head in her hands and took a deep breath.

Barb wound her arm around her in support and didn't ask more questions, but whatever happened between them, she vowed to find a way to help Lynette if she needed it.

Chapter 30

Lynette couldn't get the caller out of her mind. She'd spent so many years putting her life in the cult behind her and trying not to dwell on it that she had a hard time remembering if she'd told anyone about her aunt. A female voice, her aunt had said. Her rambling thoughts were giving her a headache.

She rinsed dishes and pans and loaded the dishwasher trying to keep her mind from wandering to Barb and their morning talk. It made her realize she still had a lot to learn about relationships, and how much she wanted to. She concentrated on her job. She'd figure out her love life later. That thought reminded her that Barb's three weeks would be up soon. Did she extend her vacation for her? She tossed that thought away and started the dishwasher.

"Hi there," Claudia said.

"Hey, Claudia. Thanks for the cookies. They were awesome."

"You're welcome. Tonight will be boring pumpkin muffins."

Lynette chuckled. "I've got all the pans ready to be filled."

"Cool. We should be in good shape." Claudia went to the kitchen to get the dinner menu finished.

Lynette walked through the dining area, using her need to check the tables as an excuse to look for Barb. She found her at her usual table smiling at her. She carried her cleaning towel and spray bottle to her table.

"Hi there. Do you have time for dessert on the balcony tonight?" Barb asked.

"Would you like to bring it to my place? Starr would love to see you."

"Sounds perfect. I'll follow you home when you get off work."

Lynette was still grinning when she went to the kitchen.

"Barb doing well?" Claudia asked.

"She is. We're going to enjoy those boring pumpkin muffins later, at my place."

Lynette filled food pans and kept an eye on them as they emptied. She couldn't remember ever seeing so many guests for dinner. She supposed it would only get worse as summer continued. She made note of the groups at the tables and kept an eye on the single individuals. Just because it was a female who'd called her aunt didn't mean that was who might show up. She took a deep breath to calm her fluttering gut and reminded herself she was safe in the middle of a busy hotel dining area. And Barb was only a few feet away.

The busy dinnertime kept her mind off the fact she'd invited Barb to her home and had no idea why. She wanted to get closer to her, but how close she wasn't sure. She recognized a shift in her comfort level with Barb. She fought a losing battle against eagerness to let her past her defenses. She finished loading the dishwasher and made a final pass through the dining area before getting her purse and going to look for Barb.

"Ready?" she asked when Barb stepped next to her in the doorway.

"Yep." Barb grinned and Lynette's anxiety eased.

She couldn't keep from checking the area before locking the car doors before starting the car.

Lynette pulled into her carport with Barb behind her. Starr wiggled her whole body when she saw Barb. "It looks like you made an impression on Starr."

The dog raced past them to her potty place and raced back by the time they were in the kitchen.

"That's important to me," Lynette said. "Starr's a much better judge of character than I am."

Lynette set the muffins on the kitchen table and filled Starr's food bowl. "Hot chocolate with the muffins?" She put two cups of water in the microwave. She was reaching in the cupboard for the hot chocolate when Barb stepped behind her and slipped her arms around her waist.

"Thank you for inviting me over. This is cozier than my balcony." She squeezed gently and stepped away.

Lynette caught her breath and turned to face Barb when she spoke. "But the balcony has a better view."

"I don't think so." Barb held her gaze. "I like this one a lot."

Lynette leaned toward her, certain of Barb's kiss and wanting it desperately, but Barb stepped back and sat at the kitchen table. She swallowed hard and retrieved the cups of hot chocolate, trying not to feel rejected. "Let's sit in the living room. It's more comfortable."

Barb laughed when Starr settled between them on the couch. "She's special." Barb scratched behind her ear and smiled when she pushed against her hand.

"Oh, yeah. You've made a friend for life," Lynette said. She didn't want to move Starr, but she would've preferred to be the one being touched by Barb. She rested her hand on Starr's back and felt the calmness it brought.

Lynette slid closer to Barb and rested her feet on the coffee table. "That's better."

Barb set her cup down, copied her position, and rested her arm over her shoulders. "This is even better."

Lynette leaned into her and Barb tightened her hold. She set her cup next to Barb's and turned in her arms. If Barb didn't kiss her this time, she planned to take control and make it happen. She respected Barb's desire for no sex and decided she wasn't ready either, but her body and soul screamed for more of her kisses. She didn't have to wait long.

Barb parted her lips slightly and pressed her lips to Lynette's. Lynette's body burned with desire, and thoughts of restraint fled. She wound her arms around her waist and lost herself in Barb. Her firm, warm lips held a slight taste of hot chocolate, and Lynette's heart pounded and her center pulsed with need. She leaned on Barb, forcing her to her back underneath her on the couch. Barb's quiet whimpers might have been words of pause or consent. Lynette hesitated for a moment to catch her breath, and Barb sat and turned to a seated position with Lynette straddling her lap. Lynette's desire smoldered. She leaned her forehead against Barb's.

"Whew," Barb muttered.

"Yeah. I sort of lost it there." Lynette grinned. "Not sorry."

Barb chuckled. "Me either."

"Would you go for a walk with me and Starr?" She moved off Barb's lap but kept a hand on her thigh.

"I'd like that, but give me a minute." Barb's hand shook as she reached for her cup and took a drink.

"Are we okay?" Lynette worried she'd pushed Barb too far.

"You are so damn sexy." Barb stroked her cheek. "You're driving me crazy. In a good way."

Lynette tipped her head and leaned into the touch as it radiated through her body to her toes. She covered Barb's hand with her own and turned to kiss her palm. "You do things to me, Barb Donnelly. Scary things." She squeezed her hand gently and stood. "Shall we walk?"

"I think I can now." Barb smiled and followed her out.

Lynette tugged on Starr's leash. "Come on, sweetie." She led the way to the one-mile trail.

"I like this path." Barb looked up at the trees as she walked and took Lynette's hand. "I'd like to ask you a question. If you don't want to talk about it, that's fine."

"Okay." Lynette thought back to what she'd already told Barb.

"You told me your aunt saved you after the cult. How did you get to her when you escaped?"

"Let's sit on that log." Lynette tugged on Starr's leash and settled on one end to leave room for Barb. She took a deep breath before beginning to speak. "One of the new kids in the group told me he and his parents had walked from a nearby town. When I ran away, I hoped his memory was correct about the direction, because that was the only plan I had. Fortunately, I made it to the town and found a pay phone. I had some change I'd sewn into the hem of my skirt along with a crumpled note with Aunt Jen's phone number on it, so I called her from that pay phone." Lynette wiped away tears, and Starr leaned onto her side. "I hadn't had contact with my aunt for twelve years, so I was afraid she might've changed her number, and I only had enough change for one call. Anyway, she drove through three states to get me. I still can't believe she found me in that tiny desert town. I'm grateful they had the name painted on their water tower. I hid in an empty barn within sight of the pay phone for the twenty-four hours it took for her to arrive." Lynette shivered.

Barb pulled her into her arms. "I'm grateful for your aunt. I can't imagine how frightened you must've been."

Lynette nestled into Barb's embrace. "I was terrified. I was certain someone would come after me, but I was so relieved to be out of there. It was the longest twenty-four hours of my life. I knew I hadn't made a mistake, but I couldn't help but feel like a traitor, too. I had a hard time acclimating to the outside world until my aunt found a great therapist for me." Lynette squeezed Barb's hand as they stood and walked back to her apartment. "I'm glad you came over tonight." She leaned and kissed her.

"I'm glad I did, too, and thank you for trusting me with your story. You're a brave woman. It couldn't have been easy to fit into a strange world."

"No, it wasn't. I had no idea what a cell phone was, or that something called the internet existed. I had a lot to learn to be able to understand what people were talking about. It's crazy how fast the world develops, and I was way behind. Claudia was helpful, too, when I started working at the hotel."

"I'm glad you're still working there, and I found you." Barb looked at her watch. "I should get back and let you get some sleep. I'll see you tomorrow at breakfast." Barb brushed her lips over hers before leaving.

Lynette watched Barb drive away and scanned the parking area before locking her door. She hadn't relived these memories in years. It reminded her of the vast differences between them. Barb grew up loved and able to pursue the life she wanted. What in the world would she want with someone so damaged by life? She had no frame of reference for her feelings, so she gave up for the night and went to bed.

Chapter 31

Barb propped herself on the bed with an extra pillow and picked up her book. She'd been back at her room for half an hour and couldn't stop thinking about the latest kiss she'd shared with Lynette. Barb longed to be the recipient of the passion simmering beneath the surface of Lynette's restraint, but she'd be going home soon. Back to the job she loved, which had caused her previous lover to leave her.

She concentrated on reading and unsuccessfully tried to quiet the voices in her head. Could she keep in touch with Lyn after she went home? Would Lyn even want to? She could return to Wisconsin on some weekends and maybe Lyn would agree to visit Michigan, but how long would that last? She wasn't one to have shallow relationships based on sexual attraction. She wanted a deep, meaningful long-term relationship, but she'd learned a lesson from Ann. Just because she wanted it didn't mean it would work out, but to never try again saddened her. Maybe she and Lyn were destined to enjoy each other's company while she was here and nothing more.

She shoved away any more heavy thoughts and went to sleep hoping for dreams of Lynette's kisses.

Barb awoke from a restless sleep and finished a cup of coffee on the balcony before showering and dressing for breakfast. She looked forward to seeing Lynette and spending time with her as she headed to the dining area. She'd allow herself that much.

The line for omelets was the shortest Barb had seen it. She sat for a few minutes to enjoy watching Lynette work. She snuck glances at her between guests, and Barb smiled at the blush that crept up her neck to her face. She finally stood and went to get her omelet.

"Good morning," Lynette said.

"Morning. It's good to see you." Barb took her omelet plate. "Do you have time for a balcony visit today?"

"I'll be there as soon as I clean up."

The heat behind her look sent desire fluttering in Barb's belly. "Great." She finished her omelet and took two muffins back to her room. She set up the coffeemaker and sat to wait. What was she waiting for? Was Lynette expecting something more between them? Had their super-heated kiss caused a shift in their feelings or intentions? Her feelings had grown, and Barb wanted to keep seeing her even after she went home. How to do that was her dilemma. The knock on the door shook her out of her reverie.

"Hi." Lynette stepped into the room and into Barb's arms. "I missed you." She stepped back before going to the balcony.

Barb brought coffee to the table between them and sat. "Have you ever been to Michigan?" she asked.

A look of confusion flashed across Lynette's face. "No, but I looked it up on my map. Why?"

"I'd like to keep seeing you after I go home. I thought maybe you could visit. If you want to." Barb took a drink of coffee and waited for a reply.

"How long a drive is it?" Lynette looked to be concentrating hard.

"It only took me about seven hours, but it depends on how fast you drive. It might take eight. Unfortunately, there aren't any direct flights."

"I'd like to, but I'll have to see if I get any vacation time. And it would only be a visit. I'm worried you want more than I can offer. I told you I can only offer friendship." Lynette frowned, clasped her hands, and twisted her fingers. "Are you leaving early?"

"No. I plan to stay another week, and you can visit as my friend from Wisconsin." Barb rested a hand on Lynette's. "Are you okay?"

"I am." She lifted Barb's hand and kissed it. "I've mostly only driven from my apartment to work and to my aunt's and back."

Barb's stomach churned when she saw the conflict in Lynette's eyes. She stood and wrapped her in her arms. "We'll work something out," she whispered.

"I'm all right." Lynette rested her head on Barb's chest and moved closer. "I get nervous driving sometimes even if I know where I'm going or following someone."

"I have a GPS unit you can have. All you have to do is listen to the lady telling you where to go." Barb's stomach settled, but areas lower began to stir. She embraced Lynette tighter.

"We'll talk about it later, okay?"

"Sure. I have muffins." Barb reluctantly released her hold. She put the muffins on the table by their coffees. "How much time do you have?"

"Plenty." Lynette spoke softly, cradled her face in her hands, and kissed her.

Barb leaned into the kiss and slid her hands under the back of Lynette's polo shirt. Her skin was soft and warm. She struggled to maintain control when Lynette moaned into her mouth. She drew tiny circles on her back before gliding her hands out from under her shirt. She rested her hands on her hips and leaned away slightly. "Whew. If we keep this up you're going to be late for work."

Lynette looked at her watch. "Yep." She cleared her throat. "I guess I better go." She didn't move. "We'll talk later."

Barb lifted her hand and kissed it before walking her to the door. Lynette had her own way of processing, and she had to respect that. And if she didn't want things to go any further, well, she'd have to accept that gracefully, too, even though she had a feeling they could have something special. If it wasn't meant to be, then so be it. But she couldn't help but hope.

After Lynette went back to work, Barb began to pace on her balcony. She recognized her unrest as pent-up energy and days of too much food. She put on her running shoes and headed outside.

Her usual day at home consisted of much more walking than she'd done on vacation, and three weeks of little activity and too many desserts had her jeans feeling tight. She ran along the river and didn't stop until she felt the strain in her leg muscles and stopped to stretch and watch the river for a minute. Her thoughts drifted to Lynette as they often did now. She wondered about the caller looking for her. Lynette was nervous about it, and frustration boiled in Barb's gut knowing she couldn't help her. She stretched again and began her run back to the hotel, having to dodge someone standing practically in the middle of the path. People could be so rude.

Barb turned up the hot water and leaned on the wall as it flowed over her body. She'd never been one to linger in the shower, but the spray trickled over her body, and her nerve endings exploded with sensation. Lynette's fingers sliding over her skin. The sweet, hungry look in her eyes that made Barb want to take her to bed and protect her at the same time. She stepped out of the shower and quickly toweled off. She would not come in the shower like some teenage boy. She wanted the real thing and challenged herself to wait until she could get it. Or to give in only when it was clear an alternative wasn't an option. She dressed and went to see Lynette, the object of her desire.

"Hey, there. I missed you at lunch." Lynette set a piece of cheesecake on the table.

"And this is why." Barb pointed to the cake. "I went for a run. I think I've gained ten pounds since I've been here."

"Do you want me to take this back?"

"Absolutely not." Barb grinned.

"I'm going to see my aunt tonight. Would you like to go with me?"

"Is she all right?"

"Oh yes. I visit her every two weeks. We get Chinese food for dinner and have a glass of wine. I know she likes you, so I'd like you to join us."

"I'd love to, but maybe you should check with her first. She might like alone time with you."

"I already did." Lynette chuckled. "She's excited to have you there. I'm going to stop at my place and pick up Starr on the way."

"Okay. I'll put this in my mini-fridge and meet you back here when you're done cleaning up." She put the cheesecake away and grabbed her jacket. She got to spend an evening with Lynette and her aunt, almost like a normal dating situation. The thought made her smile and she jogged up the stairs to her room.

Chapter 32

Lynette watched her aunt hug Barb as if she were part of her family. She allowed herself a rare sense of sadness at the knowledge her aunt was her only family. She'd met several people in her recovery group who'd had parents who'd been with them in the cults and who'd taken care of them. They missed them after they escaped. Others had parents like hers who'd abandoned them after they joined the cult. She mentally shook herself, and gratitude for her aunt filled her heart.

"I'm so glad you came with Lynette." Aunt Jen smiled at Barb.

"Thank you for letting me butt into your time with her," Barb said.

"Come on, you two. I have coffee, tea, water, brandy, and wine."

"I'll have a glass of wine if you are, please," Lynette said.

"A cup of tea sounds good with Chinese food," Barb said.

"Let's relax in the living room. You two go sit. I'll bring in the drinks and food." Jen disappeared into the kitchen and returned with her hands full. She set the cartons of various items on the coffee table and gave them each a large spoon. "There. Help yourselves to anything you'd like."

Barb stood. "You sit. I'll get the drinks."

Lynette made Starr lie next to the couch and turned to face her aunt. "Is everything quiet?"

"I think so, dear. But I thought I saw someone new hanging around my studio two days ago. I didn't recognize them and they didn't come to the door. We get new folks coming and going all the time, so it's probably nothing to worry about, but I'll keep my eye out for them."

"Could you tell if it was a man or woman?" Lynette fought down the simmering panic.

"Sorry, no. They were wearing a long coat and some sort of hat. That's why they caught my attention. It was eighty degrees outside. No need for a coat."

"Thanks for telling me. I've been sort of watching since the call, but now I'll be more vigilant. I'd sure like to know who called looking for me." Starr stood and rested her head in her lap.

"I'll let you know if I ever get another call. I promise. We both changed our numbers, so it won't happen." Jen took her hands and squeezed. "I love you, honey. You're safe now, and you have a delightful girlfriend, so try to relax."

"Barb is not my girlfriend. We're friends." Lynette didn't sound convincing even to her own ears.

Aunt Jen patted her leg. "Whatever she is, I'm glad she's in your life."

Barb returned with wine and cups and set them on the table before sitting next to her. "Thank you for all this." She rested her arm over Lynette's shoulders.

Lynette picked up her fork and a carton of food. She ate quietly, listening to her aunt and Barb talk while they ate. She felt a chill when Barb moved her arm to reach for her cup.

"This is great," Barb said.

"Aunt Jen didn't give you a tour the last time we were here."

"You're right. Come on, I'll show you where I work." Jen stood and motioned for them to follow her.

Lynette smiled at her aunt's enthusiasm. She watched Barb examine all the paintings and etchings in Aunt Jen's gallery. She sat in one of the chairs in the gallery.

"Your aunt is very talented."

"She is. I'm glad you got to see her gallery. She likes you."

"I like her, too. I couldn't dislike her since she took such good care of you." Barb lifted her chin with one finger and swept her lips over hers.

"Okay, you two. You're not alone here." Aunt Jen shook her head and smiled.

Barb stood, but before she could speak, Aunt Jen put up a hand. "Relax. But know if you hurt her, you'll have me to deal with." She wasn't smiling when she spoke.

Barb sat and grinned. "You're the second person to warn me. Claudia is just as protective. I'll bet Starr would say the same thing if she could talk." She turned to Lynette, took her hand, and kissed it. "You are well protected."

"I know, and I'm grateful. We should probably get going. Work comes early." Lynette hugged her aunt good-bye and promised to visit again soon before she followed Barb to the car. Lynette turned to face Barb before starting the car. "I hope my aunt didn't scare you. She's pretty protective of me."

"I think it's great she is. I grew up with two parents and a younger brother who were always there for me. I can't imagine how difficult it must have been to be dragged to a remote compound and expected to be an adult at twelve."

"I didn't know any different, and I didn't realize how much I missed out on until I was free. I had, still have, a lot to catch up on. You asked me about coming to Michigan to visit, and I haven't even been out of Wisconsin since I moved here. I've never been on an airplane, or taken a train or even a bus anywhere. I've read about places and countries around the world, and Aunt Jen wants to take me to the Canadian Rockies someday. To me, that feels like a world away." She rested her head back on the seat, and Starr whined from behind her. "I'm okay, sweetie." She reached back to touch her. "I better get you to the hotel."

Barb rested her hand on her shoulder the whole trip.

"I'll see you in the morning. Be careful driving home, and thank you for taking me with you."

"Sleep well."

Barb pulled her gently into a kiss so tender it brought tears to her eyes.

Lynette kissed her back with as much restraint as she could muster. She wanted Barb. More than she dared admit. Fear held her back, but she could feel it weakening with each kiss.

She took a deep breath and expelled it before beginning the drive home. "What do you think, sweetie? You like Barb, too, I can tell." Her aunt sure did. She'd called Barb her girlfriend. What did Aunt Jen see that she didn't? Where was the line between friendship, dating, and girlfriend? Her therapist had told her to try not to suppress memories of her time in the cult. She had to remember and talk about it in order to move on, so she allowed her thoughts to drift.

She'd had no idea how much she needed the closeness of another human being until Ruth began to hold her in the night. Her mother must have held her as a baby, but Lynette had no recollection of it. Neither her mother nor her father had paid much attention to her except to teach her to grow potatoes and care for the few chickens on their property. Her mother had taught her to read, write, add, and subtract, which came in handy when she was assigned as caretaker for the children in the cult. Ruth had given her what she never realized she craved. To be held by a woman in the night.

She met Donna at the hotel soon after she began working in the kitchen. She'd been free for six years, but Sarah still lingered in the background. Donna had been kind to her at first, and Lynette accepted her advances to satisfy her longing to be held. Her dalliances began a few months into their relationship, and Lynette felt a part of herself crumble with each one she became aware of. Donna finally abandoned her for one of them, and she was left broken, her trust in herself and her choices shattered.

Lynette pushed away the memories and turned her thoughts to the present. So much seemed to be happening, and fear seemed liked her constant companion again. How could she possibly have anything with Barb with her past hanging over her head? She cared too much about her to drag her into the chaos of her life. She pulled into her carport and checked the area around her car before she took a deep breath and followed Starr inside. She changed and crawled into bed with Starr at her feet. She lay staring at the ceiling debating with herself. She wanted to send Barb a note to let her know she got home safely, but it would mean she was offering her phone number. She chuckled at the thought of mistrusting Barb and grabbed her phone.

Just wanted to let you know I got home safely. Thanks for going with me tonight. My aunt was thrilled you were there. Please don't take this the wrong way, but I have to ask you to never let anyone have my number. xo L. She hovered her finger over the Send button. If she couldn't trust Barb with her phone number, how could she ever trust her with her heart? She hit Send.

Chapter 33

Barb stretched and swung her legs over the side of the bed. The sun hadn't poked over the horizon yet, but the early-morning glow highlighted the trees and river below. She stood at the door for a moment to enjoy the scene before making a cup of coffee and putting on a sweatshirt and sweatpants. She drank her coffee and enjoyed the solitude. Thoughts of her evening with Lynette brought a smile, and she looked forward to seeing her at breakfast. She checked her watch and realized she still had an hour and a half. Cheesecake wasn't technically breakfast food, but she was on vacation, and another run was definitely on her schedule. She retrieved the piece from her small refrigerator and settled back on the balcony with a fresh cup of coffee.

She unplugged her phone and automatically checked for messages, surprised that she had one. She read Lyn's message twice before replying. *No problem. Your number is safe with me. B.* She immediately marked her number as private. Her feelings for Lynette had grown as quickly as the three weeks had gone by. She remembered her mother's words: *You'll know right away when it's the right one.* But the right one, in this case, came with all kinds of complications. Were her feelings real? Or were they motivated by her romantic nature and desire to protect? Or even by the novelty of being on vacation? Was it like a summer camp crush? Or...was it simply real, and the short time span didn't matter because it was meant to be? Sometimes people knew they'd met the perfect person after a single date, didn't they? Was this any different? The moment she'd seen Lynette she'd had a wow moment, and that had only intensified over the past several weeks. It was too fast, maybe, but like her mom said, if Lynette was the right one… Her thoughts reminded her she was going to send her parents a postcard. That would be the perfect motivation for her run. She brushed her teeth, put on her sneakers, and headed out the door.

Barb ran along the river past gift shops and restaurants beginning to open for the day. She loved watching a place come awake, like the prospects of a new day were open and ready for everyone. Anything was possible when a new day began. She slowed when she reached a residential area to admire the houses and green lawns. The tree branches swayed and leaves danced in the slight breeze. When her brother had suggested this place for her vacation, she trusted his judgment. Now she was glad she had. Besides meeting Lyn, the area was a perfect mix of nature and entertainment. She picked up her pace and headed back to the hotel and Lynette.

She took a shower before going to the breakfast buffet. The room was crowded, so she hung her jacket on her chair to claim her favorite table and went to find Lynette.

"Good morning." Lynette smiled and handed her a plate with her omelet.

"Thank you. Did you sleep well?" Barb took the opportunity to talk while there was no one in line. Lynette had dark circles under her eyes. She looked tense, almost wary.

"Well enough. How about you?"

"Out like a light. I was up early and took time for a run. It's peaceful here in the early-morning hours. Thanks for the text. I appreciate your trust in me."

"It is peaceful in the morning." Lyn grinned. "You're welcome. I figured all the time and other things we've shared, my number would be a small thing."

Barb took her omelet to her table and wondered how such a short, mundane conversation with Lynette could be so interesting. She finished eating breakfast and finished her coffee while she watched Lynette work. Barb stopped by her station on her way out. "I'm going to take a walk by the river today and go to the gift shop for a couple postcards. Would you like to go with me?"

"I would. I'll come by after I'm done here, if that's okay?"

"It's perfect. See you later." Barb watched the riverboat glide down the river and relaxed with one of her romance novels to wait for Lynette. She was in the middle of a scene she'd love to imitate with Lynette when there was a knock on the door. She opened it and took Lynette's hand.

"Hi there." Lynette leaned and kissed her quickly. "It's a beautiful day. I'm looking forward to our walk."

Barb filed away the details of the scene for another time. "We can go anytime you're ready."

"Let's go." Lynette opened the door and Barb followed her out.

She held Lynette's hand on the way to the gift shop and noticed her looking back and forth before they entered the store. "Are you okay? You seem nervous."

"I'm all right. I told you about the phone call. Last night, my aunt told me she saw a stranger lurking around her art studio. Well, she didn't really say lurking, but that's what I'm calling it. It was a stranger, anyway. I'm worried about it."

"Let's go inside and look at gifts." Barb intended her suggestion to be a distraction for Lynette, but she looked around the whole shop before stepping in. "I'm looking for postcards."

"This is a nice one." Lynette held up a card with the riverboat on it.

"It is. My brother would love it."

"Here." Lynette handed her another card with the cave featured.

"Thanks. I've got my two." Barb chose one with a painting of the river. "Let's send this one to your aunt. A thank you and

• 173 •

thinking of you card. From us." Barb hoped Lynette would say yes. She liked the idea of giving something as a couple.

"I like that idea. I think she'd love it."

Barb bought all three and took Lynette's hand again when they left.

"It was nice of you to think of my aunt," Lynette said quietly.

"So, it's okay if I send it from both of us?"

Lynette stopped walking and turned to her. "She thinks you're my girlfriend."

Barb liked that idea. "Is that a bad thing?" she asked.

"No. But...I don't know." Lynette sat on a nearby bench. "I don't know. I'm so fearful that someone's looking for me, and the only thing I can think of is that it's the cult. I'm constantly looking over my shoulder. I think being anyone's girlfriend would be a bad idea."

"It's okay, Lyn. What your aunt thinks is important, but I care more about what you think." She enfolded her hands in hers.

"I told you about my past."

"Yes, you did. And it doesn't change how I feel about you."

"Barb, I'm still married to Peter, and I have no idea how I could ever get out of it."

"Do you love him?"

"You know I don't."

"He might not even be alive." Barb sat next to Lynette, and she leaned into her.

"I know. But I don't know. There are too many unknowns in my life." Lynette's tears hurt Barb's heart. "I don't understand how all this is supposed to work. I'm so confused."

Barb held her close and vowed to figure out a way to help her.

She carried the bag with the cards as they walked back to the hotel. Lynette was quiet, but at least her tears had stopped.

"Thanks for the shopping trip." Lynette headed to the kitchen. She looked tense, worried. There were clearly things she wasn't saying, and it made Barb's stomach ache. How could she battle that kind of fear? How could she help when it was something so far outside her control?

Barb walked to the post office to mail her family postcards, but she'd forgotten to get Jen's address from Lynette. She stopped to watch the river a few minutes before going back to her room. She made herself a cup of coffee and thought about what could be done. Brad could get her information about laws in Idaho, but there was no way to know where Lynette's cult had been located. From what she'd read, they sometimes abandoned their compound and took up somewhere else. Maybe even a different state. Hell, Jim Jones had moved his to Guyana. She blew out a frustrated breath. She'd have to do her best to support her and take this a day at a time. She finished her coffee and went to the dining room.

"Hi, Barb." Claudia waved her over to one of the tables.

She sat across from Claudia. "Hi. It's good to see you. Can I ask you for Jen's address? I bought a postcard for her."

Claudia leaned toward her and spoke softly. "I have it, but I have to get Lynette's permission to give it to you. I know you've already been to her place and such, but still, I have to ask. You probably know why."

It was another aspect Barb failed to take into consideration. She was going to have to learn to be more sensitive and aware. "Yes, I do. Thanks, Claudia. I'll talk to Lyn later."

Claudia smiled a knowing smile. "I'll tell *Lyn* you're looking for her." She rolled her eyes and headed to the kitchen.

Barb relocated to her favorite table and watched the people moving past the windows awhile before getting up to get her food. To her, they were people who lived in the area or were on vacation or visiting. She couldn't imagine seeing them as a possible threat. She cringed at the fear Lynette must be living with daily.

She'd almost finished eating when she saw Lynette. She smiled at her and was rewarded with a wink and small wave. They hadn't made plans to see each other later, but she wanted to. She set her empty plate aside and went to the station next to where Lynette stood. She pretended to be filling another plate as she leaned and whispered to her, "I miss you, and I need your aunt's address to mail her card. Can you stop by my balcony later?"

"Claudia's going to the market this afternoon, so I'll be over after dinner, okay?" Lynette gave her a quick smile and looked away.

"I look forward to it. I'll have the hot chocolate ready," Barb said. She finished eating and took a walk along the river to think. She'd hoped Brad would have found out something about finding bodies, but she hadn't heard from him. Even if the feds found a bunch of bodies from a cult, there probably wouldn't be any way to know which one they came from unless someone lived and told. A large part of Barb's job was helping people. Her inability to find a solution to Lyn's dilemma was tearing her up inside. She cared for her and wanted her to feel safe and happy. She sighed deeply, knowing she probably hadn't the power to make that happen. She started at the knock at the door. "Come on in," she called from the balcony.

"I brought my aunt's address."

Barb addressed the postcard and put it where she'd remember to take it to the post office the next day. "Thanks. Now everyone's covered." Barb took Lynette's hand and led her to the balcony where she had the hot chocolate waiting.

"Mmm. Thanks." Lynette took a sip, her gaze focused on the horizon.

"So, how are you doing tonight?"

"There's an important lesson my group has taught me. Take life one day at a time, and let go of what you can't control." She sighed. "It's a tough one to master."

"Know that I'm here if I can help with anything." Barb reached for her, but Lyn moved away, putting distance between them. Barb's stomach dropped at the despair in Lynette's eyes.

"I'm so sorry, Barb. I wish you could help me. I wish my life was different. I wish I could be free to do what I want, be with who I want, and live without fear. But I can't. I let myself hope we could have something deeper together, but I'm too scared. I'd potentially be putting you in danger, and I'd be constantly looking over my shoulder. I just don't see a way for it to happen. I'm going to move again, disappear and start over somewhere. You go home and live your life safely."

"Don't do this, Lyn. We can figure something out. You could come home with me if you want to move." Barb's throat constricted and her mind raced. She wanted more time with Lyn. She needed to help her. She blinked back tears and tugged Lyn into her arms and kissed her, fearing it would be the last time.

Lyn pulled away, cupping Barb's face in her hands. "Thank you," she whispered. "For being wonderful and showing me how wonderful life could be." Tears streamed down her cheeks. "I'll never forget these past few weeks." With another swift kiss, she was gone.

Chapter 34

Lynette pulled into her carport and sat for a moment to absorb the pleasant feeling after Barb's kiss. She wished she could have more with her. She wished she could be free. She locked her car, slipped her cell phone into her front pocket, and noticed a white minivan in the spot next to hers. Must be a new tenant. She returned her thoughts to Barb and how awful it felt to walk away, and how devastated Barb had looked. It couldn't be helped. She had to be safe, and this was the only way.

Just as she was about to put the key in the lock she heard a scraping noise, a footstep. Her heart pounded as she went to turn, but before she could she was slammed into the door, knocking the wind out of her. Starr was barking like crazy inside, and it was the only thing she could concentrate on as a needle slid into the side of her neck. She wanted to cry out, but the world went black.

She awoke to a throbbing headache and her feet and wrists tied by rope. Whatever she was lying on was hard and cold. She realized it was a vehicle when it began to move. Her vision began to clear, and she tried to sit up, but the rope around her waist was tied to something on the floor that held her in one spot. There was no slack in the rope so she couldn't sit up at all, but thankfully her hands were tied in front of her rather than behind her, giving her some freedom.

"Who are you? Where are you taking me?" she yelled as

panic squeezed her throat. She scanned the inside of the vehicle. The back doors were chained, as was the side sliding door. A two-wheel box carrier like the one they used for kitchen supplies at the hotel was strapped to the side wall. It must be how whoever drugged her was able to get her to this vehicle. *The minivan in the carport.* How could she have been so stupid not to see it and leave right away? She'd practically handed herself to them. She struggled with the ropes on her wrists, but pain shot up her arms when she twisted them, and there was no question of getting the knots undone in the dark. She took deep breaths in an attempt to calm herself and tested how far she could move. She could bend her elbows enough to raise her bound hands to the pocket where she'd put her phone. She could bend her knees and relieve the pressure on her ankles.

"Who are you?" she yelled again. "Why are you doing this?" She pounded the floor of the van with both feet. "Who are you?"

"Shut the fuck up, or I'll gag you, too. You're going back to where you belong." The voice was gravelly but definitely female.

"Why are you doing this?" Lynette choked out the question through tears, and there was something about the voice that was familiar. "You won't get away with it." She got no answer, so she took another deep breath and carefully moved her hands toward her cell phone. She tried to keep an eye on the driver, but the van was dark. She managed to pull her phone out of her pocket and balance it well enough to compose a text to Barb. Thank God she'd decided to give her new phone number to her after she'd changed phones. *I've been kidnapped. I'm in a white minivan. I don't know where I'm being taken but it's a woman driving. Please make sure Starr is okay and tell Aunt Jen I love her.* She'd pushed Barb away and she might have left already, so she copied the text to Claudia. She considered calling 9-1-1, but she was afraid the driver would hear her speaking and take her phone away, since she'd have to actually talk to someone. As quickly as she was able, Lynette slipped her phone back into her pocket. Her heart beat a staccato rhythm, and she forced herself not to scream. She prayed Barb would get her text and call the police. But she'd told her to go home. Tears rolled down her cheeks to puddle on the cold metal floor. She tried to wipe them away but the ropes held her hands too far away. What if Barb decided to leave that night? She'd probably wait until daylight. Barb was a brave officer of the law. She'd do whatever she could to help someone in trouble, even if it was someone who rejected her. Wouldn't she?

Lynette's mind was fuzzy with whatever the driver had drugged her with. She replaced fear with thoughts of Barb, Starr, and her aunt to keep the panic manageable. If the driver was Ruth, as she suspected, they were headed back to whatever compound they were using now. She considered options she never thought she'd need to again. If she could find sharp enough edges on the inside of the van. One swipe on each wrist, deep enough to sever whatever veins mattered. She'd have to remain quiet as she bled to death, but at least it would be over. She squeezed her eyes shut and remembered Barb's kiss. Her gentle touch. She wanted to see her again. She wanted to live. Tears streamed down her cheeks at the thought of never seeing Starr or her aunt again. The cult would probably be watching too closely for her to escape again.

"What do you want from me? Why are you doing this?" Her shouts echoed off the walls of the van.

"I told you to shut up. I am the instrument of his will. You need to fulfill your destiny. You need to finish your assignment. You will be the bearer of the anointed one's sacred children, our future. Now shut up and be still, or I'll drug you again."

Lynette's stomach churned, but she refused to throw up and show fear. *Children.* It must be Ruth bringing her back to be the mother of Brother Matthew's children. So, there must not have been a suicide event. But why in the world would he want her back after all this time? He must know she'd try to run away the first chance she got. If she banged her head hard enough on the metal floor, maybe she could bleed to death before Ruth realized what had happened. Barb's smile flashed in her mind, and the desire to live outweighed the desire to die. If nobody rescued her, she'd escape again somehow and find her way back. And maybe, this time, she could put a stop to the madness. She'd get help, find the police, and get Brother Matthew put away. She tried to shift her weight on the hard floor, but the restraints restricted her movements.

"I know who you are, Ruth. Why are you doing this? Pull over and we can talk. I know people who can help you get away. It's better outside. It's nothing like what they tell you it is."

Ruth grunted and kept driving, confirming her identity by not denying it.

Lynette tried to estimate what time it was or how long they'd been traveling, but her headache raged and her vision blurred, and time seemed to whirl around her like leaves in the wind. She closed her eyes and planned her escape. She'd win their trust. Pretend to be a devoted follower who'd lost her way and was happy to be back in the fold. Ruth was probably the one who'd called Aunt Jen, so her mother must still be alive. But how did she know where Lynette lived? A new fear tore at her heart. *What if they know about Barb?* She began to thrash and yank at her restraints until her wrists and ankles were rubbed raw. She should have been more careful. She should have moved the day after her aunt had gotten that phone call. If only she'd paid attention all those times she felt like she was being watched, maybe she wouldn't be here now. She pounded the floor of the van with her feet again in frustration.

Ruth slammed on the brakes and Lynette was thrown forward and jerked back when she reached the length of the rope around her waist. Pain shot through her ribs, forcing her to take shallow breaths. "I don't want to hear another peep out of you, bitch. Do you understand? We're going to stop for gas soon, and if you make a sound I'll slit your throat and tell Matthew you tried to kill me. Got it?"

Lynette's head ached, her throat burned, and her body felt like she'd fallen down a flight of stairs. She slumped to her side and closed her eyes.

Lynette woke to water being tossed in her face. She coughed and blinked at Ruth, who was inches away. "Drink this." Lynette swallowed the liquid Ruth fed her from a plastic bottle and immediately felt the effects of the electrolytes.

"Thank you." Her voice cracked.

"Yeah. He wants you alive, although I have no idea why he'd want a traitor like you back among the faithful. I'm sure he'll make an example of you so the others don't stray. Now, you keep your mouth shut! We're almost out of Wisconsin."

Lynette strove to clear her foggy mind. Her whole body hurt, but her heart guarded the faint hope that somehow, she'd make it through this.

Chapter 35

Her phone pinged with an incoming text and Barb grabbed it from the nightstand. She saw Lynette's name displayed and hoped she'd changed her mind, but sat up quickly when she read it. She called her brother.

"Hey, Brad. I need your help."

"What's up?"

"Remember when I asked you for info on the cults? My friend who escaped from one has been kidnapped by one of the members, and I want to know if you have a contact with any of the Wisconsin state police before I call 9-1-1 and have to do the whole runaround."

"I do. Do you know where they might be headed?"

"Idaho, I think. But I can't be sure. Her name is Lynette McCarthy." She could hear him getting up and moving around, and knowing she didn't have to handle this on her own was a relief.

"Wow. I'll give them a call and see if we can expedite something. When was she abducted?"

Barb read Lynette's text to him and gave him her name and address. "If she's beyond Wisconsin state lines, will the FBI need to be called?"

"Let's hope that's not the case. Why don't you head over to Lynette's place and I'll get back to you." Brad disconnected the call. Barb ran her hands through her hair, helplessness and anger flooding through her. She dialed the next number.

"Hi, Barb. Everything okay?" Claudia sounded like she'd been asleep.

"No. I got a text from Lynette. She's been kidnapped, and she thinks it's Ruth from the cult. I've already called my brother, who's an officer. He's making calls on his end."

"Damn. I got the text, too. Do you have Jen's phone number?"

"No. I have her address. If you give it to me I'll call her and let her know what's going on."

"Okay. Let me know if I can do anything or if you find out anything. God, I hope they find her."

"Did Lyn ever tell you where in Idaho that cult was?"

"No. Just that it was south Idaho. I think Jen knows, though."

"Okay, thanks. I'll let you know what happens." Barb put Jen's phone number in her phone, threw a few clothes into her suitcase, grabbed her keys, and rushed to her car, glad to have paid attention to the route. She parked behind Lynette's building, surprised to see her keys hanging from the lock in the door. Starr barked wildly, and her front paws were torn from where she'd scratched at the door to get to Lynette. Barb clipped on her leash, afraid she might take off in search of Lynette, and took her to her potty area.

Once she was inside and Starr was settled a little, she called Jen. "Sorry to wake you, Jen, but I got a text from Lynette earlier. She's been taken by someone she thinks is Ruth from the cult. I believe they're on the way back there."

"Oh my God, no! Did you call 9-1-1? How did she sound? Was she hurt?"

"She only texted me, Jen, and she told me she loved you. I've already called my brother, who is an officer, and I'm going to call 9-1-1 now, but I wanted to let you know first."

"I'll be right over." Jen disconnected the call.

Barb called emergency services and let the operator know

what was going on. She hoped Jen would arrive before the police and all their questions.

She called her brother next. "Hey, Brad. I called 9-1-1 about five minutes ago."

"Good. Give me Lynette's number and give it to the officers when they get there. They can follow her by GPS as long as it stays on. I'll let you know when I get any details."

"Thanks, Brad." Barb disconnected the call and took Starr to the kitchen to clean up her paws, which fortunately weren't too bad. She held on to her and pressed her face to Starr's fur. If only she'd followed Lynette home. If only she'd listened harder, been more aware of her surroundings. She couldn't let herself believe she'd lost her, not this way. She jumped at the knock at the door. She grabbed a knife from the kitchen and peeked out the curtain. Jen stood ready to knock again. Barb opened the door, and she flew past her. "You didn't need to come all the way over here, Jen. I'd have called you once I knew something."

Jen set a small overnight bag on the kitchen counter, put her hands on her hips, and shook her head. "I can see you care about my Lynette, but there was no way I was going to sit at home while she was being dragged back to that awful place." She greeted Starr and pulled out a kitchen chair to sit. "What do we know so far?"

Barb showed her the text from Lynette and filled her in on what her brother had said. "So, we wait to hear either from him or the Wisconsin police. I expect they'll contact us soon."

Jen sighed and went to the stove. "Coffee or tea?"

"Tea, please." Barb went to the door to watch for the police.

"Does your brother have any experience with this sort of thing?" Jen asked, visibly shaking.

Barb wrapped her arm around her, gently led her to the living room, and set her on the couch with Starr, who rested her head in her lap. "He's been a Michigan state trooper for years and knows members of the Wisconsin state police. He'll get the job done. You sit with Starr. I'll bring the tea in here." Barb went to the kitchen, leaned on the counter, and took a settling breath. She hated feeling so useless. She forced back tears. She'd only had three weeks with Lyn, and she wanted more. She took a cup of tea to Jen and sat across from her to wait for any news.

"I see why Lynette has fallen for you." Jen sipped her tea. "You are kind of special."

Barb forced a smile. "I'm afraid Lyn hasn't fallen for me, but thank you. She's the special one." Their conversation was interrupted by Barb's phone. She nodded as she listened to the police officer on the line. "Thank you, Officer." She disconnected the call and turned to Jen. "They're on their way to get any information we can give them. They can follow her GPS signal, but anything you could tell them about this cult might be helpful."

"It was so long ago." Jen looked to be thinking hard. "I never wanted to think about it again after it was over, but I'll do my best. She'll be okay." Jen patted her leg. "She probably told you about me going to pick her up after she escaped."

"Yes, she did. I'm grateful you were there for her."

"I couldn't believe the condition she was in when I found her. Skinny, malnourished, dirty, tattered clothes, no shoes, and sores covering her arms. But I'll tell you, she had a spark in her eye that showed me the strength beneath that messy exterior." Jen took a drink of tea. "Her mother never wanted children. She got involved with that no-good husband of hers, and the next thing I knew she was pregnant. I offered to take Lynette when she was born, but my sister swore she wanted her. There was nothing I could do but be there for Lynette when she needed me. I'm glad I was able to." Jen sipped her tea.

"She told me you were special. You are." She checked her phone and went to look out the window.

"I don't think you can see Idaho from here." Jen smiled tiredly.

"It's hard not being able to do anything but wait." Barb returned to the couch. "I want to be out on the road. I want to do...*something*." Their conversation was interrupted by a knock at the door. Barb opened it to two uniformed officers.

"We're here about an abduction call for a Lynette McCarthy."

"Come in, please." Barb opened the door wide and Jen appeared behind her.

One of the officers asked the questions while the other made notes. "So, she was taken this evening. Is that correct?"

"Yes. I found her house keys still in the door, so I'm guessing they grabbed her then." Barb showed them the text and they wrote down the information and the time it was sent.

"We'll be tracking the GPS in her phone, but tell us all you can about this cult and its location," he asked.

Jen spread her hands on her legs and shook her head. "She was taken there as a child by her parents. It's called Matthew's Faith or some such thing. They kept her for twelve years, and when she escaped she called me, and I was able to find her and bring her home." She took a deep breath and expelled it before continuing. "She called me from a pay phone and told me she was in some small desert town in Idaho. I think it was something like Weartown, or Waytown? Anyway, it was at the end of an unpaved road off Highway 93. I remember I took I-90 to get there. It was south of Twin Falls. Does that help?" Jen looked like she was ready to break into tears.

"It does, ma'am. Are you her mother?"

"I'm her aunt. Her mother is in the cult."

The officer taking notes wrote down all the information including her phone number as well as Lynette's. "Do you have a picture of your niece, by any chance?"

Jen gave the officer a picture from her wallet. "She was involved in a cult survivor's group, too. I think it met at the community center. They might know more."

"Thank you both. We'll do our best to bring her back safe." He handed them his card. "Call us if you hear anything at all." He touched the bill of his cap before leaving.

Barb watched them inspect the area around Lyn's car before

leaving. She was ready to jump out of her skin. She knew the more information they had, the better the chances of catching them, but she wanted them on the trail to finding Lyn now.

"Maybe you should try to get some sleep. They'll call when they find her. She's been gone for hours, so I imagine it'll take at least that long to get her back here," Barb said.

"I'll stay here, but I'm going to put my feet up." Jen propped herself up with a pillow and stretched her legs on the couch.

Barb took their empty cups to the kitchen and forced herself not to pace. She plugged in her cell phone and set it on the end table within reach before turning on the TV to the late evening news. "I'll be right back. I think Starr needs to go out."

Jen waved her off and covered herself with a throw.

"You know something's up, don't you." She rested her hand on Starr's back and held on to her leash when they were outside. She still worried she might take off looking for Lyn. "Your mama will be home soon." She prayed her words would make it so.

Chapter 36

Lynette woke to the scent of gasoline drifting into the back of the van. Her throbbing head and the smell caused her stomach to roil. She forced herself not to vomit, knowing Ruth would probably leave her lying in it for however long this ordeal lasted. Ruth stood outside filling the gas tank, and Lynette shifted as best she could against the floor of the van and checked that her phone was still in her pocket. She'd drifted in and out of sleep, or perhaps consciousness, and had no sense of time. It was still dark, and her bladder was full.

Ruth climbed back into the van and tossed a bottle of water toward her. She watched it roll to her side, just out of her reach.

"Could I use the restroom before we leave?"

Ruth turned and scowled at her. "I'll stop at the first rest area we come to. You'll have to hold it until then. Or not." She started the van without a second glance at her.

"Why are you doing this, Ruth? Did Matthew send you to bring me back?" She didn't expect an answer, but if she could connect with her she might find out her intentions.

"It's Brother Matthew, the anointed one," Ruth screamed. "And stop asking questions!"

Lynette ignored her yelling. "How's your little one? He or she must be at least a teenager now." She hoped Ruth would soften if she could get her to talk about her child.

"That is none of your business, you deserter. You'll find out about having children as soon as we get home."

Lynette sighed. Engaging Ruth in conversation wasn't going to be easy. She tried a different tack. "I thought he was poisoning everyone that day I left. I see you didn't die, or you didn't drink the communion wine, at least."

"Only the deceivers and hypocrites died. I am a loyal follower. I drank." She sneered as she looked in the rearview mirror at her. "Your precious husband, who you probably never fucked, didn't drink. He's dead! Brother Matthew took care of all the non-believers. Now you're coming back to service him, like it or not. Your mom and dad will be proud after you have a few of his babies. This is your chance at redemption. Brother Matthew could never forget that you ran. Now he'll be happy again. He'll be happy with me for bringing you back."

She wasn't surprised that her mother and father were still alive. They were his most devoted followers. Lynette stayed quiet until she noticed the sky lightening through the passenger side window. She'd been drifting in and out of awareness and realized the inside of the van was a little lighter. This and her full bladder indicated they'd been on the road for hours. "Is the rest stop coming up soon?" she asked.

"Yeah, yeah."

She shifted again but a sharp pain in her ribs kept her from moving much. Her stiffness was definitely going to be an issue if she tried to run. She doubted there'd be anywhere to hide in the rest area bathroom, but she had to try something. Her breath caught at flashbacks of crouching in the corner of a stall, hiding and waiting until she could be rescued. Her aunt wasn't coming this time. She was on her own, and she needed a plan.

"Why aren't you having more of his babies, Ruth?" She might be poking a hornet's nest, but she had to try to get through. If she could convince her it was better being free, she might have a chance. Once they arrived at the compound she'd never be free again.

"My babies are none of your fucking business."

"I saw a doctor on the outside. He told me about something called premature menopause."

She was taking a chance that Ruth would tell Matthew she was useless to him for babies and kill her. That would be better than being kept there as his baby maker.

"He told me it was caused from being too underweight. The diet we eat isn't enough to maintain the body fat we need to have babies. I can help you. I can take you to him and maybe you can have many children."

Ruth surprised her by pulling off the road and turning to face her. "I could have more babies?"

"Yes, Ruth. You have to follow a special diet, but you might be able to get pregnant." Lynette figured any time Ruth wasn't driving gave the police time to catch up. If, that is, anyone was coming to help.

"Where is this doctor?" Ruth looked intense.

"I can show you, but you have to take me home."

Her faced twisted and hardened. "He told me you'd try to trick me with your lies. I've seen you messing around with that woman, defying God's laws. I could have pushed her in the river that day she ran past, but I didn't want you to run off again. Just shut up, or I'll drug you again."

She turned back to face front and spun the van's tires as she pulled back onto the road. Lynette figured she was done talking, and she scrambled to think of another way to reach her. She was about to try again when Ruth swerved off the road and into a rest area.

"Come on. And no dawdling." She unhooked the rope from the van floor and dragged her out the side door.

Lynette heard her shirt tear and felt the scrape of the metal floor on her back. She took shallow breaths as Ruth pushed her to the ground and released the ties on her ankles, then yanked her to her feet but didn't untie her wrists.

"I need my hands." Lynette tried to keep her voice calm

while anger raged through her. How dare these people try to ruin her life again?

"Come on." Ruth grabbed her by her hair and pulled her like a sack of potatoes to the bathrooms. She untied her wrists and pushed her into a stall while she waited at the door.

Lynette quickly took care of business and checked the battery level on her phone. It was still ninety percent charged. In any other situation, she'd grin at the irony of the fact that she'd gotten a new phone to avoid the very condition she was in. She double-checked that the ring volume was off. She'd really be in trouble if Ruth took her phone away.

She quickly typed a short text to Barb and copied it to Claudia and Jen.

I'm at a rest stop but I'm not sure where or how long we've been on the road. I saw an I-90 sign on the highway.

She stuffed her phone back as far into her pocket as she could before rejoining Ruth. "Thank you."

"Shut up. We'll be home soon. You'll be back where you belong." Ruth tied her wrists and ankles tightly with zip ties this time, but didn't tie her down to the floor.

Lynette leaned against the side of the van opposite the door and bent her knees. The position was more comfortable, but her back burned from the scraping and her shirt stuck to the bloody abrasion. The vantage point gave her a better view out the passenger side window, and she watched the sunshine grow brighter.

It had to be at least twelve hours since she'd been abducted. Where were the police? Hadn't Barb called them? Was she already home? Claudia should be up by now and heading to work. She leaned her head back and closed her eyes.

The van stopped moving and Lynette blinked to clear her vision. The throbbing in her head had eased and been replaced by soreness throughout her body. Her stomach growled and Ruth was gone. She leaned forward as best as she could to see out the windshield. They were at another gas station, and her stomach lurched at the sign on the building. They were in Wyoming. This was the end, she was sure. Another few hundred miles and she'd be trapped again in the clutches of Brother Matthew. She had to get away.

Chapter 37

"I got another text," Barb told Jen who'd been dozing on the couch. "She sent it from a rest stop somewhere off I-90."

"That's all she said?" Jen asked.

"Yes. I've already sent it on to the police." Barb set her phone on the end table. "At least we know she's alive and not to the cult yet. Maybe that's all she had time for if Ruth's watching her."

"Why haven't the police found her yet?" Jen stood and began to pace.

"I don't know. Ruth did get a head start on them." Barb joined in the pacing. "Ruth has committed a federal offense by kidnapping Lyn and taking her across state lines. She'll be going to prison for a very long time." Barb wanted to ease Jen's anxiety as much as her own. They had to catch her first. "Why don't you go lie down in the bedroom? I'll come get you as soon as I hear anything."

"I doubt I'd be able to sleep. I'm fine here."

Barb grabbed her phone when it rang, hoping for word about Lyn. "Hi, Claudia."

"Hi, Barb. I just wanted to let you know I got a text from Lynette from a rest stop."

"Yeah, I got one, too. We know she's alive."

"So, you haven't heard anything from the police yet, huh?"

"No, but Ruth had quite a head start. It's been over twelve hours, so I'm hoping we'll hear from them soon." Barb sat on the couch to keep from more pacing.

"Well, let me know, and I'll let you know if I hear from her again. Oh, and Barb?"

"Yes?"

"Thank you for being there for her. She's a good friend and a good person who doesn't deserve the kind of life she's had."

"No, she doesn't." Barb disconnected the call and leaned back on the couch. She glanced at Jen, who'd dozed off again. She never would have considered not helping Lyn even though she'd sent her away. *What if I'd left last night?* She knew she'd have turned around and come right back, but was that what Lyn wanted? Lyn was scared of exactly what was happening now. It was her fear that had pushed her away, and Barb planned to do whatever necessary to bring her home safely. If she still wanted her to leave after that, she would.

❖

Ruth slid back onto the driver's seat and turned toward her, and Lynette stared into her sad eyes. "What now, Ruth? Are you sure you don't want to come back with me and see that doctor? Nobody would stop you if you wanted to go back to Brother Matthew afterward." Lynette hoped to reach Ruth before it was too late. It would only be a few hours before they reached the compound.

"I don't want your fucking doctor. You're a traitor. A deceiver. An apostate."

"Then why, Ruth? Why does Brother Matthew want me back?"

"He needs babies to follow his teachings. His legacy. I don't know why he'd choose a non-believer like you, but I think he'll be pleased that you're back in the fold, and getting children from you would make your redemption complete. I could give him more children, I know I could, but he rejected me because I didn't give him a son. I tried again but he told me my womb was dry."

"The doctor might help you. Won't you try?"

"You are a liar! Now shut up. We're almost there. I suggest you start remembering your teachings so you please him when we arrive."

Lynette remained quiet and formulated her plan. She'd escaped once as a weak, immature, sickly young woman. She'd had a taste of freedom and love, and she'd never give that up. Thoughts of Barb and her gentle touch and warm kisses kept major panic at bay. She would return to her and honestly let her know how she felt about her. Somehow she'd find a way out of that cult or die trying. She closed her eyes and meditated while waiting for the inevitable.

The rocking of the van threw Lynette to the opposite side of the van. Her shoulder hit the door handle and she cried out in pain. She braced herself as best she could but her vision blurred and went black from the force that rolled her back, and she hit the other side of the van.

Yelling and crying filtered into Lynette's consciousness before awareness of the pain throughout her body. Ruth seemed to be in some sort of distress, and the van definitely wasn't moving. She tried to sit up but a sharp pain in her shoulder sapped her strength. She turned carefully until she could see out the passenger window. Blue and red flashing lights blinded her for a moment, and she realized the yelling was mixed with sirens. A sliver of hope gave her strength to call out, and the van's side door was torn open. The daylight streaming freedom into the van was the last thing she remembered before darkness took over again.

❖

Barb's ringing phone startled her awake. She rubbed her eyes, frustrated that she'd fallen asleep, and snatched her phone. "Hello, this is Barb."

"Is this Barb Donnelly?" a male voice asked.

"Yes." Barb had no patience for this. "Is this about Lyn? Have you found her?"

"This is Sergeant Williams from the Wisconsin police department. We have Lynette McCarthy. She's safe but pretty banged up. She's agreed to medical treatment but only if we bring her to the hospital near her home. We have a medical transport on the way."

"Thank you, Sergeant."

"It'll be at least ten hours until we get back."

"Couldn't you use your lights and sirens?" Barb paced as she spoke.

Sergeant Williams chuckled. "That's the plan, but Wyoming is pretty far away. We'll make sure she's secure before we call you for a time to debrief. One more thing. The driver of the van was a member of that cult, and the feds are making her take them to the compound. They'll take over the case from here."

"Thank you. We'll be here." Barb settled on the couch and disconnected the call. She gently squeezed Jen's calf to wake her. "They have her, Jen. Lyn is safe and the FBI is making Ruth take them to the cult compound. I think Lyn is free."

"Thank God." Jen stood and stretched. "Coffee or tea?"

"Coffee, please, but I can make it." Barb smiled at Jen's solution to any situation. She stood and Starr jumped off the couch to stand next to her.

"I need to move a little. My neck is stiff from lying on the couch."

"Okay." Barb texted Claudia to let her know what happened.

"Come on, Starr." Barb hooked on her leash and took her outside. She sat on the outside chair and tried to unwind after the tense hours. Starr finished and sat by her side. "Your mama's on

• 197 •

her way home. When she gets here, I'll take you to see her. She'll like that."

How would Lyn feel about seeing her? She'd told her to go home. She was willing to let her walk out of her life forever. What about now that the cult threat was over? If the FBI descended on the cult, would they shut it down because of the kidnapping? Did that mean Lyn would be truly free?

"I don't know what to think, Starr, but I know I'm going to be here when she gets home."

❖

Lynette awoke with a tube attached to a needle in her arm and a bag of fluid hanging next to the bed. She listened to the quiet hum from a machine with lights and numbers flashing. She knew she was in a hospital, and she hoped it was the one she'd asked the officer to take her to. Her aunt had brought her here for what she called routine tests when she'd escaped from the cult. This discomfort was minimal compared to the fear and torment she'd just endured from Ruth, and she wished Starr was with her. Grogginess took over and she dozed until hushed voices woke her.

"You can see her, but don't be too long. She's extremely dehydrated and needs to rest," the nurse on duty said softly.

"Thank you."

"You'd think I was half dead the way people tiptoe around here." Lynette didn't try to hide her delight at seeing Starr. The fact that Barb was with her gave her goose bumps.

"Well, I see you're feeling well enough to joke." Barb smiled.

Starr rested her head on her arm, and a huge piece of the angst she'd been carrying since she'd been abducted fell away. Barb looked amazing except for the uncertainty in her eyes. Lynette knew she was responsible for that but was in no shape to change it. "I'm probably in shock."

"I don't think the doctor mentioned shock. Dehydration and some other injuries, but no shock." She grinned and Lynette reached for her hand with her free one.

"I need to thank you for saving me."

"I wasn't the only one involved. Your aunt Jen would have found a way to get you, and Claudia got your text, too. You were well covered. Did anyone tell you the good news about Ruth?"

"I hope it's that she's in prison for the rest of her life."

Barb grinned. "I'm not sure what sentence she'll get, but she led the FBI to the cult compound. They raided it, Lyn. I don't know all the details about it, but you're free. Whatever happened out there, it's over. And I promise that if I hear anything else, I'll tell you right away."

Lynette didn't even try to stop the tears. Finally, tears of joy. It would take time for everything to sink in, but the news was salve to her wounds. She reached for Starr and rested her hand on her back. "Thanks for bringing Starr. Has she been okay without me?"

"She was frantic when I arrived at your place, but she settled down when Jen got there." Barb took her other hand and kissed it.

"Hey, am I too late for the party?" Jen asked as she entered the room with a huge bouquet of flowers. She kissed Lynette on the cheek and set the flowers on the window sill.

"Thanks. The flowers are lovely. I don't think I'm up for partying just yet, though."

"Did the doctor say how long you'll be here?" Jen asked.

"Not to me." She looked at Barb.

"They wouldn't tell me much. Not related. Jen can find out what's what."

"I shall return with information." Jen left and turned toward the nurse's station.

"Were you with Aunt Jen the whole time I was gone?"

"Yes. I went to your place as soon as I got your text and she arrived shortly after."

"She looks tired. Did she get any sleep?"

"She dozed on the couch, but I couldn't get her to go to bed." Barb shrugged.

Lynette decided to just ask the question on her mind. "Are you going back to the hotel now that I'm back?"

"Is that what you want?"

Lynette's answer was interrupted by the return of her aunt. "I have news." She looked happy. "You have a mild concussion and a fracture of the *something something* bone in your shoulder. You're dehydrated, and your back is all scraped up." She grinned.

"Well, that doesn't sound too bad. Can I go home now?" Lynette wasn't sure she could stand, let alone get dressed and go home.

"No. But maybe tomorrow, if you're not there alone, and if you do nothing but rest and heal. They have to change the dressing on your back now, so we should probably leave." She looked at Barb. "Did you tell her the good news?"

"I did. She's free," Barb said.

Lynette gave Starr one last big hug and kissed her aunt goodbye. She really wanted a kiss from Barb, who'd smiled and squeezed her hand, and maybe, now that things had changed, she had some choices to make.

Chapter 38

Barb filled her suitcase with her remaining clothes and double-checked the closet and bathroom. She went to the balcony for one last look at the river below. She'd enjoyed every minute of her stay here, and the fact she'd shared it with Lynette made it even more special.

She checked the time. She'd offered to stay with Lyn until she was healed enough to be on her own, and Barb hoped it wouldn't be uncomfortable for them. She took one last look at the view before heading out the door.

"Hey, Claudia." Barb leaned her suitcase against the wall by the door.

"Hi there. I'm sure glad everything turned out all right with Lynette. It must have been so terrifying."

"Yeah. She's pretty banged up, but she'll be out of the hospital this afternoon."

"Do you think she'd be up for a visit tonight? I'd like to stop by after work."

"She'd love to see you. Jen is picking her up from the hospital, and I'm heading to her place now. I'll text you if Lyn isn't up for visitors."

Claudia held up a finger and went to the kitchen. She returned carrying a paper bag. "Here are a few of my special muffins for you guys."

"Thank you." Barb wrapped her in a hug. "I'm glad Lyn has you for a friend." She grabbed her suitcase and rolled it out to her car. Pondering her future was never anything Barb spent much time on. She loved the profession she'd chosen and had convinced herself she wasn't lonely. Since meeting Lyn, she'd become aware of a hollow place that she craved to fill. She didn't know how this vacation would end, but she knew it would. She'd either be going home to continue her life alone, or Lyn might decide she was worth trying for more than friendship with. Either way, she'd need to call her chief soon. Jen's car was in the parking lot when she arrived at Lyn's.

"Hello," she called from the doorway. "I come bearing gifts." She set the bag of muffins on the counter and went to look for Jen and Lyn.

Jen looked up from the side of the bed. It was obvious she was trying to tuck the covers in around Lyn, who was pulling them out from the end of the bed.

"Need help with an unruly patient?" she asked and grinned.

"My toes are sore, Aunt Jen. The covers are too tight. And I hate sleeping on my stomach."

"I see you must be feeling better, grouchy one." Barb helped Jen tuck the side covers in and pulled out the bottom so they were loose for her feet. "Better?"

"Thank you." Lyn looked contrite. "I'm sorry. You guys saved my life, and here I am bitching at you about bed sheets."

Jen chuckled and gave Lyn a kiss on her cheek before waving Barb to follow her out of the bedroom. "These are the instructions the hospital sent Lynette home with. I made this chart," she held up a piece of paper as she spoke, "for all her medications and treatments."

Barb looked at the list and nodded. Jen had used her artistic skills to map out a daily schedule with a spot for checkmarks as they were done. "Thanks. This makes things easy. So, how is she, really?"

Jen sighed. "She'll heal physically, but her PTSD was severely triggered and may take time to let up. The doctor prescribed something to help her sleep, and Starr hasn't left her side. I know my niece is a very strong young woman. She'll get through this."

"I'm glad she has you to help." Barb took Jen's hand and squeezed gently.

"As far as I'm concerned, she's my daughter. I'd never refuse to help her. I'm going to head home for a while, but I'll be back later to check on her. Call me if you need anything."

"Sounds good, and thanks again, Jen."

Jen waved as she left, and Barb went to check on Lyn. "How are you feeling? Can I get you anything?"

"I don't think so. I'm kind of groggy but I think I remember I owe you an answer. It's no." Lynette shifted a little and closed her eyes.

Barb had no idea what Lyn was mumbling about, but she wasn't going to press her for anything while she was so woozy. She looked so vulnerable, and Barb's heart ached for the terrifying ordeal she'd gone through. She lightly stroked her cheek before leaving the room.

Barb unpacked her suitcase and hung a few items in the spare bedroom closet. She added her toothbrush and some toiletries to the collection on the bathroom counter and retrieved a towel from the small bathroom closet. She gazed at herself in the mirror and reflected on the past three weeks. She'd enjoyed a relaxing vacation, met an incredible woman, helped save her from a crazy cult, and now she was standing in Lyn's bathroom wondering if she should stay or go home. It wasn't like Jen couldn't take care of Lynette just fine. But she couldn't bring herself to go.

She took a quick shower and put on clean clothes before going in search of something to make for them to eat. She was rummaging through the cupboards when Jen knocked on the front door. She let her in and swooned at the delicious scent from the box she carried.

"I brought pizza. I know Lynette loves it, if she's up to eating, and I hoped you did, too."

"Oh, yes. I was just looking for something to make. This is perfect. Thank you."

"How's the patient?" Jen set the pizza box on the table.

"She was sleeping when I peeked into her room a few minutes ago. I'll go see if she's hungry."

Jen followed her to Lyn's room. Lyn was sound asleep, and Starr lay with her head resting on her leg.

"Let's let her rest," Jen whispered. "We'll save her a couple pieces for later."

Barb led the way back to the kitchen and put plates and napkins on the table. "Thanks again for thinking of this." She took a bite of pizza.

"I'm really glad you were able to stay longer. Do you have a deadline to be back to work?"

"I need to call my chief and let him know how much longer I'll be, but I wanted to see how Lyn was progressing before I do that."

"I see." Jen swallowed her bite of pizza and remained quiet.

"I plan to stay as long as she needs me," Barb said softly and rested her hand on Jen's arm. Apparently, her subconscious had made the decision for her. So be it.

Jen smiled and looked relieved. "That's good. That's very good."

"Get some rest tonight. I'll be sure to call you if something changes with Lyn. And thanks for the great chart you made. It'll help me keep track of things."

After Jen left, Barb reviewed Jen's chart and sorted the medication. She set the alarm on her phone as a reminder to give Lyn her antibiotic in an hour and checked on her before turning on the TV and settling on the couch.

She woke to the dinging of her phone. She took a glass of water and Lyn's pills to the bedroom, pleased to see her awake and talking quietly to Starr. "I have your antibiotics for you," she said from the door.

Lyn rolled to her side and sat up on the side of the bed. Her huge grin indicated she was pleased with herself at the accomplishment. "I can't swallow those lying down."

"I'm glad to see you feeling better. How's your back feel?" Barb knew changing the dressing was next on her list of items to do. It wasn't exactly the way she'd imagined seeing Lynette without her top on the first time.

"It's sore, which is better than painful like it was." She swallowed her pills and finished the glass of water.

"I'll refill your water glass and be right back to change the dressing on your back." Barb stepped out of the room and leaned against the wall. Lyn's beautiful blue eyes had lost the pain-filled haze and sparkled when she smiled at her. They were going to have to talk. Barb had feelings for Lyn far beyond friendship and knew it would be a struggle to keep them to herself. Her need to keep her safe and care for her warred with her desire to gather her in her arms and profess her feelings. She'd nearly lost her, and that thought shook her to her core. She took a deep breath and concentrated on the task at hand. She washed her hands, collected what she needed, and returned to find Lyn lying on the bed face down. She'd removed her pajama top, and Barb gazed at the soft swell of her breasts as they pushed against the bed underneath her. She mentally slapped herself. Lyn didn't need her lusting after her.

"I'm going to remove this bandage now." She pulled back the dressing and carefully removed it. The skin was rubbed raw, but there were no deep lacerations. Most sections were scabbed over, and the healing process had begun. She used the antibiotic cream the hospital had provided and covered the abrasions with a sterile dressing.

"This looks pretty good. You're healing already." She couldn't stop herself from lightly caressing Lyn's bare shoulder before taking the supplies away. This was going to be harder than she thought.

Chapter 39

Lyn put her top back on when Barb left the room, and she trembled slightly from the gentle sweetness of Barb's touch. She pushed herself off the bed, noting where things hurt and where they didn't. The places where Barb had been felt distinctly nicer.

Barb returned with her full water glass, and Lyn stood next to the bed bracing herself with her hand on the wall.

"You must be feeling better." Barb smiled and stood close.

"I had to see if I could do something besides lie in bed all day."

"No dizziness?" Barb asked.

"No. And thank goodness my head doesn't throb anymore." She sat back down on the side of the bed. "I'm hungry, though. All I could keep down in the hospital was some awful soup." Lyn stepped slowly toward the kitchen.

"You stay here. Jen brought some pizza. Think you could handle a piece?"

"Please." Lyn sat back on the bed and rested her hand on Starr's back. "I'm so glad to be home." She allowed the tears to flow as the memory of what had happened replayed once again. Gray walls, flashing lights, and a face full of hatred made her weak inside.

"Here you go." Barb returned with the pizza and handed Lyn the plate. Their fingers brushed, and the contact felt like a jolt of electricity radiating up her arm. Barb sat next to her on the bed and gently wiped away a tear from her cheek. "Are you all right?"

The need to be held was hampered by her sore shoulder, so she set her plate on the nightstand and kissed her. Her lips were warm and soft and welcoming. She whimpered when Barb deepened the kiss and ran her tongue over her lower lip, then whined when she pulled away. "Why did you stop?" She tried to slow her ragged breathing.

"I don't want to stop, sweetheart. I just can't keep kissing you and feeling you everywhere and then be sent away. It's tearing me apart." Barb stood and ran her hand through her hair.

Lyn had sent her away to protect her. Had she lost her now that she was free? "We need to talk." She took a bite of her forgotten pizza and swallowed before speaking. "I'm sorry if I hurt you. Exactly what happened was what I was afraid of. It could have turned out very differently, and I could've been trapped again. What if you had been here and they'd hurt you to get to me? I couldn't take that chance, and I care too much about you to put you through that." She rested her hand on Starr and took a deep breath. "But if the threat of Brother Matthew is over, will you forgive me and stay?"

Barb gathered her in her arms and Lyn's fear dissolved. "Finish your pizza, and I'll get you a cup of hot chocolate."

"Is that a yes?"

Barb took her hand and kissed it. "I have to check in with work in a couple of days, but I'm not going anywhere right now except to get your food."

"Thank you." She kissed Barb again before she could leave. "Is there more pizza?"

Barb chuckled. "I'll bring two pieces."

If her back wasn't so sore she'd flop back on the bed. She settled for practicing standing and sitting a few times. Starr watched her every move but didn't jump off the bed. Her vision was clear, and the horrendous headache was gone. She'd heal, and soon she'd make an appointment with her therapist. She closed her eyes and allowed the delightful feeling of being called sweetheart by Barb to wash over her.

"Here you go." Barb walked in carrying a tray with a plate of pizza slices and two cups of hot chocolate. "I thought I'd join you. This is probably dinner unless Jen brings something else. Oh, I almost forgot. Claudia might stop by tonight."

"Great. I'd love to see her." Lynette took a huge bite of pizza and swallowed before sipping her hot chocolate. "Yum. Thank you. This is perfect."

"I'm glad you're feeling so good. If you're up to it after we eat, we can put your arm sling on and sit on the couch and watch the news. Jen will be over later."

"I'd like that. I'm pretty sick of being in bed." Lynette hoped Barb would call her sweetheart again. She set her plate and cup down and stood. "Am I supposed to wear that sling thing all the time? Because I'm going to the bathroom."

Barb retrieved the sling and she slipped her arm into it, surprised at how much pressure it took off her shoulder. "It feels pretty good, actually. I'll be back." She kissed Barb quickly before grabbing some clean clothes and walking out of the room.

"I'll be right outside the door. Call if you need help," Barb said.

The view in her bathroom mirror surprised Lynette. She had bruises on her arms, legs, and right cheek. Her shoulder was swollen, sore, and bruised, and her hair was a mess. She hoped to be able to wash it but couldn't get under a shower with her back bandaged. She settled for brushing it, sponge bathing, and putting on clean clothes. She felt more human when she walked out of the bathroom. "I'm pretty beat up, aren't I?"

Barb smiled and stroked her cheek. "Yeah, but you're tough. You'll heal."

"Yes, I will." She took advantage of Barb's strength and leaned on her as they went to the living room. She eased onto the couch and Barb left to let Starr outside and feed her.

"Claudia gave me some muffins earlier. Do you want one now, or with coffee tomorrow?"

Lyn looked at her incredulously.

She grinned and shook her head. "Okay. I'll get them now."

"Hello. I'm coming in," Jen called from the door.

Lynette rose gingerly to greet her. "Look how good I'm doing." She hugged her with her good arm, and a sense of rightness washed over her. She had Barb here, and her aunt and Starr. Gratitude filled her heart.

"You are. I brought a casserole for you guys and some fresh zucchini bread." Jen put her foodstuff in the refrigerator.

"Tea?" Lynette asked.

"Thank you, dear. But I can make it."

"I need to prove to myself that I'm healing and able to do more than sit around."

"Fine. I'll go say hello to Barb." Jen left the room shaking her head.

Lynette managed to make a cup of tea for her aunt and carry it out to the table next to the couch. "See what I can do?" She settled next to Barb, unwilling to admit how tired she was, and her dull headache had returned.

"I got a call from Claudia while you were making tea. She's going to stop by tomorrow, if it's okay with you. She worked late tonight."

"I hope she's not overworked without me there. Maybe I'll feel up to going—"

Barb and Jen spoke in unison. "No."

Lynette tried to keep up with the conversation, but Barb felt so warm and soft, and her arm around her shoulders begged to be cuddled into. She closed her eyes for only a moment.

Chapter 40

"Are you absolutely certain?" Barb asked her brother, needing the information he gave her to be true. He'd called to see how Lynette was feeling, and he had news about the cult.

"I am, sis. My lieutenant confirmed it for me, and you've met her. She doesn't mess around. She talked to an FBI agent and the Department of Corrections as well as the prosecuting attorney. The cult woman goes by the name Ruth, and she had no ID on her. They couldn't find her prints in the system and suspect she might've been born in the cult. Her appointed attorney is working out a plea deal in exchange for information. Anyway, she's in prison with a lighter charge for the felony of kidnapping Lynette across state lines. You already know the feds raided the cult compound. They tried to take the leader into custody, but he shot at them with an automatic weapon, so they killed him. They found an arsenal in a storage room. The surviving adults and children were taken away for questioning, but a few of the adults were found dead. They think it was suicide. I'm not sure what will happen to the survivors. I suppose they'll be free to go wherever they want if there was no abuse proved."

"How did your lieutenant get all this information?"

"She 'knows people,' is all I got out of her."

"Thanks for letting me know." Barb disconnected the call and checked on Lyn. She found her sleeping, so she made herself a cup of tea and ate a muffin while she debated calling her chief or just returning home and talking to him in person. Her future had never been unclear before. Now she knew she wanted it to include Lyn, but how that would work was her dilemma. Lyn was healing well and getting stronger. She wouldn't need Barb there in a few days, not physically anyway. But she would probably need emotional support for a good while. Barb quit her pondering. They'd talk when Lyn woke up. She took her tea outside to sit on the patio and enjoy the sunshine and blue sky.

"Good morning." Lynette sat on the chair next to her, and Starr settled on the ground in front of them.

"Glad you're being good and wearing your sling."

"It reminds me not to try to use my sore arm too much. Did you sleep well?"

"I did, but how are you sleeping? I checked on you about midnight and you looked comfortable." Barb didn't share her desire to crawl into bed with her to hold her and make all her pain go away. She admitted to herself that was impossible but her desire to try stuck with her.

"I took a pain pill last night. I don't like the way they make me feel, but my shoulder ached."

"Good. You take them when you need them. You won't need them forever." Barb stroked her arm lightly. "I got a call from Brad this morning."

"Yeah?" Lyn turned to face her.

Barb told her all Brad had said and kept her gaze on Lyn's face to make sure she was handling it okay. She leaned to kiss Lyn and took her hand. "You really are free, sweetheart."

"You know," Lyn looked thoughtful, "Ruth wasn't a bad person. I tried to talk to her when we were in that van. She just wanted to have more babies for Matthew. She was upset with herself, like it was her fault her body betrayed her. I think I almost connected with her, but she was so programed to believe everything Matthew said that she couldn't hear me. I offered to take her to my doctor, but she didn't believe a word I said."

"There was probably nothing you could've said to her to earn her trust. She was brainwashed by a charismatic narcissist."

"Yeah. It's too bad. I wish...I wish I could have saved her, you know? But she could have gotten away, the same as I did, and I have to remember that." She swiped at her tears. "I'll bet my parents were some of the suicides. They would have died for Matthew. He and the cult were their whole life. They wouldn't have anything else to live for."

"I imagine you'll be notified if the FBI finds their bodies."

"Maybe so. I'm getting a cup of coffee. You want one?"

"Yes, thanks." Barb refrained from offering to help, recognizing the need for Lyn to feel capable of normal activities.

"Here you go." Lyn came outside, set Barb's cup on the table next to her, and went back into the building. "And here's mine." She sat back down and sipped her coffee. "It's nice out here."

"I'm glad you're doing so well." Barb took a drink of coffee.

"Me, too. I'm getting good at doing things one-handed, but my shoulder feels much better. So, what's happening with your job? Are you going to have to go home soon?"

"I'll probably call Jake, he's my chief, tomorrow and see what's happening. But I wanted to talk to you first."

"I don't want you to leave." Lyn stood, and Starr went to her side. "I...don't want you to leave. Come on." She grabbed Barb's hand and led her into the apartment and to her bedroom. "Please lay down with me?"

Barb hesitated but wasn't going to deny Lyn anything. She pulled her into her arms on the bed and sighed. "I'm not going to leave and never come back. I'm hoping we can figure out a way to be together, and I hope you feel the same way." She rolled to her side and made sure Lyn's bad shoulder was protected before she kissed her. Lyn surprised her by pushing her to her back and lying on top of her. Her thigh slid between her legs and pressed against her center, and Barb shivered with need.

"Oh, sweetheart, wait. I want this more than anything, but I want us both to be healthy because I don't want to hold back or worry about hurting you." She trembled and took deep breaths until her body settled.

"Sorry, love. I got carried away. I just wanted to cuddle and talk." Lyn moved off her but slipped her arm out of her sling and rested it across her waist. "I wanted to make sure you weren't going to leave me."

Barb held her gently and kissed her again. "I want you in my life forever. Is that what you want, too?"

"Yes. I can't imagine living my life without you. I was so scared in that van that I'd never make it back to you, that I'd never see you again or kiss you again. Thinking of you was a huge part of how I got through it."

"I'll call my chief tomorrow morning, but I may have to go back to work for a while. Then I want us to really talk and plan our future. I love you, Lyn. I was so scared I'd lost you to that cult and I'd never get to tell you how I felt." Her stomach clenched at Lyn's tears and she snaked her arm underneath her and pulled her close. "Please don't cry. It'll all work out."

"These are tears of joy. I never believed I'd be free, much less find someone to fall in love with. Someone who loved me, too. Ruth and Donna both betrayed me, and I decided there had to be something wrong with me. For the longest time I wondered if Matthew was right and I was only unhappy because I wasn't going with the program. I guess I expected some magical feelings I could call love." Lyn trembled and Barb lifted her hand to her lips. "I need you to understand. I don't want any question about the truth of my love for you. My aunt told me recently true love can't be forced or denied, and I don't want to deny myself true love. I want you in my life forever. I love you, too."

Chapter 41

Lynette prepared two bowls of oatmeal and poured two cups of coffee, happy to feel closer to normal. Pleasantly surprised at the result of the exercises the doctor had suggested, she needed her sling less every day. Her range of motion in her shoulder might never be the same, but the pain and swelling had disappeared. As she set the table and waited for Barb to get out of the shower, she reflected on how much their lives were about to change and how much she looked forward to it. Barb would be heading to Michigan to request a transfer to an area closer to the Wisconsin border, and they'd spend time talking when she returned. She smiled when Barb stepped into the kitchen running her fingers through her damp hair.

"Thanks for making breakfast." Barb drew her against her and kissed her.

Her body hummed with arousal as their breasts met. She slid her hands under her T-shirt and skimmed her fingers on the underside of her breasts. She loved how sensitive Barb was to her touch, but she knew there wasn't time for what she had in mind for her. She asked anyway, "Do we have time for more before you leave?" She trembled with need.

"Sorry, sweetheart, it's a long drive and I told Jake I'd be in his office before five." Barb kissed her one more time and sat at the table. "I promise I'll make up for it when I get back." The smoldering look she gave her confirmed her intentions.

"I'll miss you." Lynette hated that she sounded whiny, but they'd spent the past two days in and out of bed touching and kissing and exploring each other and talking about their future together. She'd found real love and a vision of a limitless future, so she resisted separation from that even for a couple days. But Barb had obligations and would return. She repeated the thought several times. "I'm going to work later to help Claudia in the kitchen." The thought of returning to a familiar routine helped settle her anxiety.

"Be careful. Make sure you take your sling even if you don't think you'll need it. And I'll miss you, too. I'll text or call you every day." Barb shoved a spoonful of oatmeal in her mouth. "Are you going to talk to your therapist today?"

"I am. I have an appointment at nine. She's going to give me names of schools to check into. I'm excited about starting classes. I appreciate your suggestion to look into becoming a licensed therapist to work with cult survivors. I think it's something I'll be good at, even though it might be hard sometimes."

"You told me you connected with Ruth during your ordeal. I bet you'd be good at therapy work." Barb looked at the clock. "I better get going. I love you and I miss you already. And when I get back we'll do planning. Hug Jen for me." Barb stood and wrapped her arms around her. She kissed her one more time before grabbing her suitcase and leaving.

Lynette sat at the table to finish breakfast and pondered how she'd become so entwined with Barb. When she was gone, Lynette felt as if a part of her had gone with her. She sighed, knowing Barb was on a mission to make a way for them to be together. She cleaned up the breakfast dishes and took Starr and her coffee outside.

"What do you think, Starr? Would you like to move? The only thing I'll miss about this place now is how close it is to Aunt Jen." Her car was in the same spot it'd been since the fated night Ruth had come for her. She shuddered at the memories. They no longer threw her into panic, but she hoped they wouldn't linger much longer. "I have a lot to discuss with my therapist today, girl. Come on. We've got time for a walk."

She relaxed as they took the familiar path and the PTSD that had a hold of Lynette for so long began to melt away. Ruth and Brother Matthew were gone. She could live her life the way she wanted to, with love and peace. She could have any future she wanted and never have to look over her shoulder again. Not only that, she could help people who had been through the same thing. The future felt impossibly beautiful, and she wanted to gather the feeling of joy in her arms and squeeze it to her.

She checked the time when they arrived back at her apartment and hurried to take a shower, looking forward to seeing Claudia and immersing herself in familiar work. She dressed, headed out the door, and settled into the comfort of familiarity as she drove. It would take time for her to ignore any white minivans, but she embraced the feeling of freedom as she drove. She'd lived with unrest her whole adult life, and she reveled in the knowledge she could choose her future, and it would include love. She pulled into the hotel parking lot and smiled all the way into the building.

She found Claudia filling pans in the kitchen. "Hi, Claudia."

"Lynette." She rushed to gather her in her arms and carefully hug her. "I'm so glad to see you're okay. Are you sure you're up to working today?"

"Oh yes. I have an appointment at nine, but I plan to be back afterward." She stepped back to enjoy the warm reception from her friend. "I'll get the dining area ready."

"I'd appreciate that. I'll carry the pans out when I get them ready—and, Lynette?"

"Yeah?"

"It's really great to have you back."

"Believe me, it feels great to be back. I have lots to tell you. We'll talk later, okay?"

"Definitely."

Lynette worked steadily until it was time for her to leave for her appointment. "I'll be back in a couple of hours," she told Claudia.

"See you then." Claudia waved from the kitchen where she stirred a pot on the stove.

Lynette stood outside the hotel for a moment, surprised at her automatic reflex to scan the area for danger. She took a deep breath and strode to her car. Healing would take time, but she knew it would happen. She checked her phone for any word from Barb before starting her car. She probably wouldn't call or text while she was driving, so Lynette sent her an *I love you* text before starting her car.

She arrived at her therapist's office a few minutes early, so she checked her phone and smiled. A text from Barb. *I love you, too.* She had plenty to talk about today, so she locked her car and headed inside.

Chapter 42

Barb arrived at Jake's office with an hour to spare. She sat in her car for a moment to organize her thoughts. She'd told him over the phone that she wanted to make a location change but hadn't given any specifics. She took a deep breath and went to his office.

"Welcome back." Jake smiled and stood.

"Thanks." Barb would miss him and their easy camaraderie. "I need to talk to you, if you have time?"

"Of course. Sit." Jake pointed to the chair in front of his desk. "You look serious. Are you all right?"

"I'm fine. I wanted to let you know I've requested a transfer to Escanaba. I wanted to tell you in person before you got my paperwork."

"Damn. I didn't see that coming, but I'm sure you have good reason." Jake shuffled papers on his desk. "Did something happen on your vacation? If you need help with anything, you know you can count on me."

"I know. Thank you." Barb had never come out to Jake, but she always thought he suspected her sexual orientation. She wouldn't hide who she was. He could potentially make her life miserable, but she was transferring out of his area. "I met someone." She deliberated how much more to say, but Jake interrupted.

"Ah. I understand. If you remember, I came to this post from downstate years ago. I was happy where I was, but my chief sent me up here for temporary duty until more recruits came on board. It's where I met Esther. I requested a permanent transfer after two weeks and we were married six months later. You're very good at your job, and I know you love it." Jake stood and offered his hand across his desk. "I'm proud to have had you on my team, but you have to follow your heart."

Barb blinked back tears and shook his hand. "Thank you, Jake. I'm proud to have served on your team. Will you have enough personnel if I leave immediately?" Barb hoped she didn't need to commute for long.

"Yeah. You go do what you need to do. I've got two officers and four recruits up to speed."

"Thanks again. I'll keep in touch." Barb meant her words. She'd worked with Jake for ten of her eighteen years as an officer, and she valued his leadership.

"One more thing, Barb." Jake grinned. "Congratulations."

"Thank you." She saluted before leaving his office. She took a breath once she got to her car. She hadn't expected any resistance from her chief, but his personal disclosure touched her deeply. She stopped at the Realtor's before heading to her house. She didn't know how she and Lyn would work out their lives together, but she knew she wanted to, and knowing what her house was worth was a sensible step.

She pulled into her driveway, turned off her engine, and leaned her head back on the headrest. A sense of loneliness flashed over her. She missed Lyn. She grabbed her suitcase and entered her small two-bedroom cabin. The deck overlooking the woods was perfect for relaxing with a morning cup of coffee and watching the birds. She filled the feeder and went inside to send Lyn a text before beginning the process of sorting items to take back with her.

I'm home. All is well here except I miss you.

Lyn probably wasn't home from work yet, so she put her

phone on the kitchen counter and began making a list. Lyn's text interrupted her list making.

Things are good here except that I miss you! Did it go well with your chief?

Barb smiled at the memory of how sweet Jake had been.

It went well. I'll be able to transfer immediately. Therapy go okay?

Barb waited for a few minutes and made herself a cup of tea. Lyn's text came within ten minutes.

Therapy was great. I can't wait to show you all the info I got. I miss you.

I'm glad it was great. I look forward to seeing it all. Kisses.

She picked up her paper and pen and continued room by room. She finished her list and took it to her deck with her tea to watch the birds before dinner and reflect on her life since meeting Lyn. She'd expected a vacation with relaxation and communing with nature, and here she was willing to sell her house and move in order to be with someone she'd fallen for. Unexpected, but perfect. She checked her cupboards and freezer, happy that she didn't need to run to the store. She made a peanut butter sandwich and another cup of tea and returned to her deck.

After her meal, she did a load of laundry and organized what she'd be packing in her Jeep and settled to watch TV. She sent another text to Lyn.

I sure wish you were next to me watching TV.

Her reply was immediate.

Me too. I doubt we'd be watching TV, though. Hurry home, love.

Barb took a hot shower and crawled into bed. Her thoughts drifted to Lyn next to her, vulnerable and trusting, soft and warm, gentle and loving. Her last thought as she fell asleep was how terribly much she missed her.

The next morning she awoke and automatically reached for Lyn. She sat up disoriented and remembered where she was. She got up and made some coffee and scrambled eggs before texting Lyn.

Morning, sweetheart. I sure missed you last night. And now.

She sat on the deck and finished breakfast before beginning the process of loading her Jeep. She fit as much as she could into it and locked the door to the house before leaving.

Barb took one look back at the place she'd call home for ten years and pulled out of the driveway toward Lyn. She'd miss it here, but home was where Lyn was, and they had new memories to make together.

She followed the highway toward Wisconsin but turned off halfway there. She pulled into the parking lot of Harlow's by the Bay and hopped out of her jeep and into a hug from her friend Josie.

"It's great to see you. How was your vacation?" Josie tugged her into the lodge.

"It was great to get away for a while." Barb followed her into the large common room of the lesbian resort she'd opened two years ago. "Actually, it was fantastic." Barb sat on the chair facing the huge fireplace, and Josie sat across from her.

"Something to drink?" Josie asked.

"I'm good, thanks. I've got a long drive ahead of me."

"A long drive? Okay, spill it, and I want details." Josie grinned.

"I met someone while I was vacationing, and she's amazing."

"Wow. That sounds serious." Josie frowned, then rose and pulled her into a hug. "I'm happy for you. So, what's her name? When are we going to meet her?"

Barb smiled at her friend's enthusiasm and noted her knitted brow. "Her name's Lynette, and I see your expression of concern."

"Well, I'm just hearing about her now, but you've only known her for what? A month?"

"I appreciate your voice of reason. She works at the hotel where I stayed, so I saw her every day. We spent time together talking and doing things." She smiled at the memory of how hard it was to get Lyn to open up and how close they'd become. But sharing the details of what they'd been through didn't feel right, not without Lyn's consent. "I realize that everyone's different and no two relationships are alike, but you knew when the time was right for you and Kelly, didn't you?"

Josie laughed. "She knew it before I did, but I think I know what you're trying to say. Yes. I remember the feeling when I knew she was the one for me. I'm happy for you."

Barb chuckled. "I'm on my way back now." She looked at her watch. "I wanted to stop and let you know what was going on though. One more thing. I'm transferring to the west side area. Near Escanaba."

"That's not *too* far. We'll still get you see you sometimes." Josie squinted at her. "We better. Kelly will be sorry she missed you. She's at the assisted living center visiting my grandmother."

"Tell her I said hi, and I'll bring Lyn over as soon as we have a plan in place. I promise." She hugged Josie again before leaving.

Barb drove out of the parking lot toward the main road and let her mind wander. She'd grown up and lived her life in the area except when she was away at college. She expected to feel a loss at the anticipated upcoming changes in her life, but instead joy and contentment filled her heart and pushed away any lingering loneliness. She smiled and pointed her car toward the expressway and Lyn.

Chapter 43

Lynette put the tablecloth on the table and two candles before setting the plates and silverware out. She added wine and water glasses and checked the time. Barb had called to let her know she was half an hour away, and Lynette wanted everything to be perfect. She checked the Cornish hens and stirred the rice before taking the salad bowl out of the refrigerator. She grinned when she heard Barb pull into the parking lot, then she smoothed out the short red dress she'd bought for this occasion and waited for Barb to walk through the door.

"I'm home." Barb opened the door and stopped in the doorway. "You look stunning." She dropped her suitcase on the floor and gathered her in her arms.

"I'm glad you're home." Lyn kissed her with all her pent-up desire and shivered when Barb slowly ran her hands under her dress and discovered her panty-less state.

"Oh, God. You are so hot." Barb's breathing was ragged as she stroked her soaked pussy and Lyn's knees buckled. Barb held her tight and never stopped stroking until she slid one finger inside her. Lyn rode her finger and hand until she felt her orgasm unfurl and take over her control. She clung to Barb, pumping against her hand, feeling her finger curl to stroke her inside, and she buried her face in her neck, shuddered, and cried out as she came again.

"I'm so glad you're home." She lightly nibbled Barb's neck, then kissed it. "I made dinner." Her voice cracked.

"I'm starved. Starved for more of you, that is." Barb cupped her bare ass and lifted her to carry her to the bed. She stripped off her shirt and nearly tripped stepping out of her jeans.

Lynette loved to have Barb naked. She lifted off her dress and tossed it to the floor before she pushed her back on the bed. Barb's nipples were extremely sensitive, and she tickled one with her tongue. Barb writhed under her touch and moaned when she sucked one nipple, then the other. She bucked on the bed and grabbed the sheets when Lyn slid two fingers through her wetness and inside her. She pushed Lyn's hand harder against herself, and Lyn watched her orgasm take over. She was gorgeous. She flopped back on the bed, and Lyn cuddled into her when she wrapped her arm around her.

"Mmm. Shoulder?"

"What shoulder?" Lyn kissed her, then smiled. "It's more tender than sore or painful. I'm healing." Barb was her salve, the healing balm for her heart, body, and soul. She smiled against her breast and flicked her nipple with her tongue to hear Barb whimper. "I made Cornish hens and rice. Are we going to eat dinner?" Lyn's bleary mind and sated body told her to close her eyes and sleep. Dinner could wait.

"You went through all the trouble to make it, so I think we should eat. I can tell you about my trip." Barb pulled her closer and kissed her before sitting and swinging her legs over the side of the bed.

Lyn traced her fingers down Barb's bare back to her ticklish spot, which produced more whimpering from her lover. She'd spent most of her life without control, so to have such an effect on someone so strong and loving delighted her. "Okay. Let's eat so we can get back here soon." She kissed her shoulder and climbed out of bed.

Barb dressed and headed to the kitchen, so Lyn took her time dressing. She slipped back into the little red dress, hoping to keep Barb distracted enough to get her back to bed soon, but chose underwear for her own comfort.

Lyn found the wine poured, salad dished out, and their plates full when she sauntered to the table. She smiled at Barb, who looked at her like she was definitely going to be dessert.

"So, tell me about the info you got on classes?" Barb asked and took a bite of food.

"Sonia, my therapist, gave me a list of schools to check out. Many have online classes, so maybe I wouldn't have to commute too much. We talked about my abduction and all the cult stuff." She shivered at the memories and took a sip of wine. "I told her about you and how happy you make me." She took a bite of food and realized how hungry she was. She swallowed and sipped her wine, ready to speak when Barb interrupted her by placing her hand gently on her arm.

"I want to make you happy, sweetheart, but more than that, I want you to be happy with yourself. If you're happy with who you are, there'll be room to be happy with me." She kissed her lightly and picked up her fork.

"You sort of sound like Sonia. It's scary." She grinned. "I still have to work through my PTSD, but she told me to be proud of how far I've come. I'm working on it."

"I'm proud of you. It can't be easy getting through that." Barb took another sip of wine. "I stopped at a Realtor's office on my way north."

"Yeah?" Lynette watched Barb carefully. They hadn't made any future plans, but she knew she wanted to.

"I wanted to get an idea of what my house might be worth. I doubt you'd want to move too far away from Jen, but I'm not sure I like the idea of staying in an apartment." Barb took another bite of food and looked thoughtful.

"You're right about Aunt Jen, and I'm not sure where I'm going to school." Lynette pushed down the rising panic she recognized as her fear of change. She loved Barb and she wanted a life with her. The cult was gone and she was free to live her life wherever she wanted to. Wherever they ended up, she wanted it to be together. "I want us to be together."

"Me, too. I put in for a transfer to an area on the border of Michigan and Wisconsin, so I can commute from here, if that's what you want. Too many changes at one time could be pretty stressful."

Trust Barb to understand her need to take things a piece at a time. "I think I'd like to do that for now, if you'd be okay with it." She motioned to the apartment with her fork. "But I was thinking while you were gone, and I'd like to leave this place at some point. You've made it better, but now it holds some memories I don't want to share space with."

Barb's face lit up with a beautiful smile. "As long as I'm with you, it'll work. We'll take our time and find a house we both love that's also near a school for you. It'll be perfect."

Lynette nearly wept once again, but instead she pushed aside her meal and led Barb back to the bedroom. Perfect was exactly the right word.

Epilogue

One year later

"Are you almost done, love? Aunt Jen will be here any minute," Lynette called from her seat underneath their covered patio. She rested her hand on Starr's back and grinned as she sipped her hot chocolate. She still had to pinch herself occasionally to verify this wasn't a dream. She was safe in her own home, married to the wonderful woman who now leaned over the flowing water of their newly installed pond. She watched her fiddle with something while straddling the water.

"I'll be right there." Barb stood, turned, and held up her tools in a victory stance. Her eyes never left Lynette as she strode toward the house. "All set. It needed a new filter." She leaned to skim her lips over Lynette's before she settled in the chair next to her.

The water flowing in the pond wasn't the Wisconsin River, but Lynette could hear it from her vantage point. The creek adjacent to their property, and the bird feeder next to it, nestled among the trees, gave the yard a park-like feel.

"Have I told you I love you yet today?" Lynette scooted her chair closer to Barb's so their arms touched.

Barb rested her arm over her shoulder and squeezed gently. "You tell me every minute of the day with your smile and your touch, but I sure like hearing it. I love you now and forever."

"Hey, you two honeymooners. I hope you've got your clothes on." Jen appeared from around the corner of the house, and Starr rushed to greet her. "I knocked on the front door before I saw your note to come to the back. Wow." She took in the yard and set a present on the table before hugging them both and petting Starr. "This is very nice. You guys did good getting this place."

"We've been working on it all spring, whenever I'm not studying and Barb isn't out saving the forest." Lynette clutched her cup to keep from tearing open her aunt's gift. "Can I get you a cup of tea or something?" she asked.

"In a bit, honey." Jen moved the box to Lynette's lap before sitting at the table.

"I'll be right back." Barb went into the house and returned with a pitcher of iced tea, glasses, and a plate of cheese and crackers. "We've got coffee or hot tea, if you'd prefer, and of course, hot chocolate." She grinned.

Jen poured herself a glass of iced tea. "Thank you." She looked at Lynette as she spoke. "It's a good thing you had sense enough to marry this one." She lifted her glass toward Barb.

"I know. Believe me, I know." Lynette smiled at Barb from her seat. She took a deep breath and wrenched her focus away from the gift in her lap.

"I'm pretty sure I got the better end of this deal." Barb looked at her phone. "Brad and Angie aren't going to make it. She's having contractions, so they're headed to the hospital."

"I thought she wasn't due till next month," Lynette said.

"She's not, but I suppose babies sometimes decide when they want out."

"I guess it's just us." Lynette looked between Barb and Aunt Jen. "Claudia had to work, but she might stop by later. I hope to hear about her new executive chef position."

"So, open it." Jen pointed to the box.

She ripped off the wrapping paper with tiny houses all over it and tore open the box. "Oh, Aunt Jen, it's beautiful." Lynette carefully lifted the rainbow-colored hummingbird feeder from the box filled with Styrofoam pellets.

"Wow. It is," Barb said.

"It's my first attempt at working with glass." Jen grinned and sipped her tea.

Lynette gently set the feeder back in the box and stood to pull her aunt into a hug. "Thank you. I love you."

"Yeah. Thank you so much." Barb joined in the group hug.

"You are so welcome." Jen looked out at the yard after disentangling herself. "It's peaceful back here."

"We like it that way." Lynette leaned on her aunt with her arm around her waist, Barb on her other side. "Peaceful and quiet."

She smiled and relaxed in the knowledge she was home, safe, and loved. The past was well and truly gone, and she was living her truth—love's truth, one of acceptance, adoration, and beauty.

About the Author

C.A. Popovich is a hopeless romantic. She writes sweet, sensual romances that usually include horses, dogs, and cats. Her main characters—and their loving pets—don't get killed and always end up with happily-ever-after love. She is a Michigan native, writes full-time, and tries to get to as many Bold Strokes Books events as she can. She loves feedback from readers.

Books Available From Bold Strokes Books

Fleur d'Lies by MJ Williamz. For rookie cop DJ Sander, being true to what you believe is the only way to live…and one way to die. (978-1-63555-854-8)

Guarding Evelyn by Erin Zak. Can TV actress Evelyn Glass prove her love for Alden Ryan means more to her than fame before it's too late? (978-1-63555-841-8)

Love's Falling Star by B.D. Grayson. For country music megastar Lochlan Paige, can love conquer her fear of losing the one thing she's worked so hard to protect? (978-1-63555-873-9)

Love's Truth by C.A. Popovich. Can Lynette and Barb make love work when unhealed wounds of betrayed trust and a secret could change everything? (978-1-63555-755-8)

Next Exit Home by Dena Blake. Home may be where the heart is, but for Harper Sims and Addison Foster, is the journey back worth the pain? (978-1-63555-727-5)

Not Broken by Lyn Hemphill. Falling in love is hard enough—even more so for Rose, who's carrying her ex's baby. (978-1-63555-869-2)

The Noble and the Nightingale by Barbara Ann Wright. Two women on opposite sides of empires at war risk all for a chance at love. (978-1-63555-812-8)

What a Tangled Web by Melissa Brayden. Clementine Monroe has the chance to buy the café she's managed for years, but Madison LeGrange swoops in and buys it first. Now Clementine is forced to work for the enemy and ignore her former crush. (978-1-63555-749-7)

A Far Better Thing by JD Wilburn. When needs of her family and wants of her heart clash, Cass Halliburton is faced with the ultimate sacrifice. (978-1-63555-834-0)

Body Language by Renee Roman. When Mika offers to provide Jen erotic tutoring, will sex drive them into a deeper relationship or tear them apart? (978-1-63555-800-5)

Carrie and Hope by Joy Argento. For Carrie and Hope, loss brings them together but secrets and fear may tear them apart. (978-1-63555-827-2)

Detour to Love by Amanda Radley. Celia Scott and Lily Andersen are seatmates on a flight to Tokyo and by turns annoy and fascinate each other. But they're about to realize there's more than one path to love. (978-1-63555-958-3)

Ice Queen by Gun Brooke. School counselor Aislin Kennedy wants to help standoffish CEO Susanna Durr and her troubled teenage daughter become closer—even if it means risking her own heart in the process. (978-1-63555-721-3)

Masquerade by Anne Shade. In 1925 Harlem, New York, a notorious gangster sets her sights on seducing Celine, and new lovers Dinah and Celine are forced to risk their hearts, and lives, for love. (978-1-63555-831-9)

Royal Family by Jenny Frame. Loss has defined both Clay's and Katya's lives, but guarding their hearts may prove to be the biggest heartbreak of all. (978-1-63555-745-9)

Share the Moon by Toni Logan. Three best friends, an inherited vineyard, and a resident ghost come together for fun, romance, and a touch of magic. (978-1-63555-844-9)

Spirit of the Law by Carsen Taite. Attorney Owen Lassiter will do almost anything to put a murderer behind bars, but can she get past her reluctance to rely on unconventional help from the alluring Summer Byrne and keep from falling in love in the process? (978-1-63555-766-4)

The Devil Incarnate by Ali Vali. Cain Casey has so much to live for, but enemies who lurk in the shadows threaten to unravel it all. (978-1-63555-534-9)

Secret Agent by Michelle Larkin. CIA Agent Peyton North embarks on a global chase to apprehend rogue agent Zoey Blackwood, but her commitment to the mission is tested as the sparks between them ignite and their sizzling attraction approaches a point of no return. (978-1-63555-753-4)

Journey to Cash by Ashley Bartlett. Cash Braddock thought everything was great, but it looks like her history is about to become her right now. Which is a real bummer. (978-1-63555-464-9)

Liberty Bay by Karis Walsh. Wren Lindley's life is mired in tradition and untouched by trends until social media star Gina Strickland introduces an irresistible electricity into her off-the-grid world. (978-1-63555-816-6)

Scent by Kris Bryant. Nico Marshall has been burned by women in the past wanting her for her money. This time, she's determined to win Sophia Sweet over with her charm. (978-1-63555-780-0)

Shadows of Steel by Suzie Clarke. As their worlds collide and their choices come back to haunt them, Rachel and Claire must figure out how to stay together and, most of all, stay alive. (978-1-63555-810-4)

The Clinch by Nicole Disney. Eden Bauer overcame a difficult past to become a world champion mixed martial artist, but now rising star and dreamy bad girl Brooklyn Shaw is a threat both to Eden's title and her heart. (978-1-63555-820-3)

The Last First Kiss by Julie Cannon. Kelly Newsome is so ready for a tropical island vacation, but she never expects to meet the woman who could give her her last first kiss. (978-1-63555-768-8)

The Mandolin Lunch by Missouri Vaun. Despite their immediate attraction, everything about Garet Allen says short-term, and Tess Hill refuses to consider anything less than forever. (978-1-63555-566-0)

Thor: Daughter of Asgard by Genevieve McCluer. When Hannah Olsen finds out she's the reincarnation of Thor, she's thrown into a world of magic and intrigue, unexpected attraction, and a mystery she's got to unravel. (978-1-63555-814-2)

Veterinary Technician by Nancy Wheelton. When a stable of horses is threatened, Val and Ronnie must work together against the odds to save them and maybe even themselves along the way. (978-1-63555-839-5)

BOLDSTROKESBOOKS.COM

Looking for your next great read?

Visit BOLDSTROKESBOOKS.COM
to browse our entire catalog of paperbacks, ebooks,
and audiobooks.

**Want the first word on what's new?
Visit our website for event info,
author interviews, and blogs.**

Subscribe to our free newsletter for sneak peeks,
new releases, plus first notice of promos
and daily bargains.

SIGN UP AT
BOLDSTROKESBOOKS.COM/signup

Bold Strokes Books
Quality and Diversity in LGBTQ Literature

Bold Strokes Books is an award-winning publisher
committed to quality and diversity in LGBTQ fiction.

CPSIA information can be obtained
at www.ICGtesting.com
Printed in the USA
BVHW070820080321
601990BV00005B/251